X

OUT OF THE BLUE

A story of a young man's journey from
the palms of the Vietnam jungle to the
forested pines of far west Oregon.

KEN PALMROSE

Out of the Blue by Ken Palmrose
Copyright © 2021. All rights reserved.

Published by Pen It! Publications, LLC in the U.S.A.
812-371-4128 www.penitpublications.com

ISBN: 978-1-954868-13-7
Cover Design by Donna Cook
Edited by Leslee Mackey

Table of Contents

PREFACE

This is Ben's story as he hops aboard the Greyhound on a journey from his home near Sisu Bay, a coastal resort in Oregon to one of the most rural areas of the West. He had recently returned from Vietnam where he served for over 14 months. But this will be a different journey and involve different 'wars'. Wars such as forest fires, murder accusations, and other life-changing events.

Besides a story of the beginning of a young man's real-life journey, this book is also a reminder of the nightmares and daydreams of being in a war zone; some bad, some good, but memories that are forever lurking in the mind's shadows.

This book is dedicated to hard working men and women who help manage and protect America's natural resources. It is also dedicated to those Vietnam Veterans whose stories are seldom heard. The soldiers who were not on the front lines out on a LRP, or defending some soon-forgotten jungle mountain top for the third time, or flying a gunship under enemy fire, but rather to the vast majority of those who never fired a single round. It is about one young man's journey from 'the jungle palms to the western pines'. Follow Ben as he embarks on a long bus trip from the coast to a new beginning of what he hopes will the start of a life-long career.

CHAPTER 1

Ben looked around at the dark half-full bus thinking to himself, "What the hell am I doing, leaving home, heading east on this 'gray dog' to nowhere?"

With thoughts of returning home from Vietnam and the warm welcome of his family still there, he knew it was now time to get back into the world and begin a career journey that many would envy. He looked forward to starting his job in forest management and hoped for many years to follow, a career perhaps. Ben reminded himself that this is his first real fulltime job that actually pays a decent wage. If things work out, he will go from a partial full-time employee to one that is completely fulltime, thanks to his Veteran's status. As the bus headed away from the Sisu Bay, God, he thought, I sure hope this is all worth it as the bus ride was already boring and a little uncomfortable. Ben stretched across any empty row of seats toward the back of bus. It felt a little hot and clammy and the hard-worn leather seats did not make much of a bed. The trip to his new job was going to take all night-long only to end up in a town that is smaller than his neighborhood back home.

But Ben was very much looking forward to working in the Blue Hills National Forest rather than in the woods as a logger like most of his family and it is his very first job since graduation from his two-year college class in Forestry. Since finishing the two-year program and his time in the Army including 14 months in 'Nam', things are finally looking up, he thought.

But this bus ride, Ben thinks to himself, Jesus, what a group of characters I get to ride with and get a peek at that old guy up front he thought to himself. The older guy Ben saw was in his late 70's or early 80's and had a scraggly beard, a well-worn dirty-brown baseball hat covering his stringy white hair. In his arthritic old boney hands, he held a paper bag with some kind of a booze bottle peeking out once in a while. Ben watched him closely and every time he unscrewed the bottle cap from deep inside the crumpled brown bag, the whole bus started reeking of cheap wine. 'Super chicken' reigns once again or Mad Dog perhaps. Whatever it was, it made heads turn every time the old boy took a hit.

The good news about this particular bus ride, Ben reminded himself, was that he changes buses in about three hours in Centerville, maybe he will get to ride with some normal people, a better clientele, he thought.

****

4

Geez Ben thought, now the guy behind me is snoring like crazy and the couple in front may get arrested for what they are doing. Ben couldn't help noticing the couple two rows in front of him. A young hippie-looking guy with long black hair and a short beard nuzzling up next to a beautiful young redhead who appeared to be a lot younger, perhaps not even of legal age to be with a dude as old as he looked.

I am not a prude Ben thought to himself, but crap, they both need to take a cold shower.

Ben could see them through the opening in the seats in front of him as the guy snaked his hand up her skirt. The young redhead practically held her long cotton skirt open like my old Grandma's front gate in invitation.

The couple started making out like they were at home as Ben and everyone else could see these two touch touching parts of each other that usually never see the light of day.

"Shit," Ben said to himself, "Let's get this bus moving a little faster so I can transfer to the Trailways for the last half of the bus ride and I don't have to watch this!!"

"Look at those two," the guy behind Ben whispered, "if he gets her any more undressed, I am heading up front."

Ben began to doze off thinking to himself, I do not care how dark and crappy and uncomfortable this old bus is, how did I get stuck with this group. I have no desire to know these two people that closely. I don't think the slogan 'leave the driving to us,' pertains to these idiots. Besides this bus is damn small, and between the smell of wine and these two sweating all over each other, it is already a long ride.

"*However,*" Ben smiled and thought to himself, "*I will say they definitely are a little more athletic between the seats than anyone else on the bus.*"

Ben looked at the older gentleman driving the bus and immediately began to remember the first time he saw someone like him, a Negro, or a Black man as some liked to be called. Ben grew up in an essentially all-white coastal resort where there was only the occasional Chan and Rodriquez thrown in. But, getting drafted changed all that. This bus driver reminded him of another bus driver, the one who took the newly sworn-in draftees to the old North Fort section of Fort Lewis. He was also a Negro and he too always had a big smile and friendly hello.

****

Ben's exposure to someone who didn't look him took an interesting turn. Memories of basic training flooded in as he remembered being greeted by a stern and athletic-looking young Black Drill Instructor name Sgt. Wiford. This man could yell out a dozen consecutive orders without ever taking a breath and he was only five foot nine. He had everyone lined up, gear in hand, marching off to their barracks in a matter of seconds and scared shitless, which of course was one of his sole purposes in basic training life.

Ben remembered quite vividly his eight weeks of basic training. And the one thing that still haunts him the most was during the fourth week of basic. They had been learning to march like real soldiers out on the parade grounds just outside their barracks front door.

Sgt. Wiford yelled out to his trainees a stern warning, "Listen up you little cry-babies and pay attention to what I am about to tell you! No one, I repeat no one is to go more than halfway across these parade grounds. That post half-way at both sides marks as far you can go. You also are not to go anywhere but your barracks and the dayroom unless I give you permission. You can go as far the parade grounds halfway posts."

No one really understood the why of this order until two evenings later.

That is when Ben heard another recruit blurt out, "Look over there across the parade grounds by those other barracks. What the hell is going on?"

Ben looked out the window of the day room and watched as men in some kind of strange military gear could be seen hauling bedding, mattresses, and other items into a huge pile. There must have been at least a 50 mattresses along with blankets, sheets, and other items. And then, on command from one of the officers, gas was poured onto the pile and the entire mountain was set on fire. The flames, even in the misty weather reached a hundred feet high. By now almost everyone in the barracks had piled into the dayroom and up to the windows.

Another recruit followed up stammering, "What the hell is going on, does anyone have a clue?"

Sgt Wilford, who had been standing in the doorway responded in an oddly somber voice, "Look I may as well tell you as it will be on the news anyway. The reason we are confined to our barracks or this day room and have to use half the parade grounds is because of a serious disease outbreak that is occurring here and on other military posts. It appears there were several confirmed cases of spinal meningitis in those barracks over there. Everything must be decontaminated, cleansed, burned or whatever it takes to make ensure those barracks and grounds are safe for training once again. There were five members of one training platoon taken to the hospital two weeks ago. I do not know their condition, if they were infected or even if they survived. This disease can be devastating and deadly, so you girls damn well remember, it is an order to stay the Hell away."

****

The bus hit a small pothole and Ben slowly started to wake up after his brief doze-off and another bad dream about his service time. He seemed to be having more dreams or memories of his brief military service. He remembered thinking back then, what if I don't even make it through boot camp, because some did not.

About a half hour later, a fully awake Ben could see a light up ahead as the bus approached Centerville and he could finally switch buses for the rest of the trip. Even though he dozed off once a while, his constant reoccurring dreams kept him tired, especially since it was now right around 1:00 a.m.

"Holy crap look at that dump we are stopping at, that is the worst looking old cafe I have ever seen!" a passenger up front exclaimed. "Damned if I am going to eat anything they are serving!"

The one lone light outside the run-down café appeared to be the only light working in the whole village, and it was drawing every single moth for a hundred miles. It looks like Centerville is indeed dead center in the state, but this place is also definitely dead and almost abandoned as in no-wheresville as the café, gas station, and a run-down motor hotel and a few ramshackle house were it, the whole town.

As the 15 or so passengers stumbled sleepily off the bus for their middle of the night rest-stop, the old dude that drives the bus unloaded the suitcases for those transferring to Trailways for the continuation of the trip east, another four or five-hour journey.

What Ben didn't realize was that the next leg of this journey would only take around two and half-hour drive in anyone's family sedan, but not this particular bus trip. The bus, he has now figured out, slows down for a thousand curves, stops at every single village and gas station, and will wander up and down hills and mountains once again for the next five hours. Only a dozen stops, more or less, and then his long sleepless journey would be finally over.

Ben followed the old geezer who finally ditched his brown paper-bag somewhere along with the young couple who managed to untangle themselves and wander into the rundown café. The café held two rows of three tables. They were hand-made picnic tables with wooden benches on each side and the tables were covered with 'table-clothes'. Well, they weren't exactly table-clothes at all, but rather some kind of fancy-grade off-white butcher paper tacked down. They all looked like they had been there for more than one sloppy meal, as they were all stained with ketchup drops, brown coffee cup rings, and a dead bug or two.

Out of nowhere, the owner, came out from the tiny little kitchen and flipped several one-page menus on each table like he was dealing bad poker hands. Ben took one look at this supposed 'cook' and marveled how he could envision this guy as the cook in Chaucer's Canterbury Tales, one of his favorite classics from HS English. The cook sported matted brown hair which was a crumpled greasy mess. Ben had no doubt he probably just rolled out of bed or a cot of some kind from somewhere in a back room. This fat old guy, with his dirty apron barely hanging over his over-sized waist could have been right out of the novel, large sores on his face and all.

The menu had a few sandwiches and hamburgers and fries and a couple choices of soft drinks and shakes. The hippie-looking dude whispered to his young girlfriend, "I am not eating anything that greasy-looking fat slob touches."

She looked at him and whispered back, "Shh, he might hear you and I don't think he would like to hear you calling him those names."

He ordered her a bag of chips and a coke for her and a 7-Up for himself since He was glad all the pop came in a can rather than from the filthy stained soda fountain.

Nobody ate much, mostly ham and cheese sandwiches with warm mayonnaise and mustard. Several commented about how they hoped they didn't get food poisoning; but they were all too tired and hungry to care. The passengers who were travelling on eastward departed the café as quick as possible with only a few of them gambling on a late-night unsanitary sandwich. The thought of getting sick on a bus winding through the mountains was not a pleasant thought.

****

As he climbed sleepily onto the Trailways for the last part of the trip, Ben noticed how few passengers were continuing on. What a difference the new bus was, it smelled better and rode ten times smoother. Everyone started stretching out in their own row of seats settling in for a little snooze. Much better, he thought as he once again began to doze off to sleep, or at least off and on sleep.

Too bad for Ben, the time for sleeping didn't last, as the bus wandered down the highway winding sharply to the left and then to the right and up and down a half-dozen or more hills, through deep canyons, and up and over small mountain passes making sleep broken and uncomfortable as the bus swayed on every hairpin turn, and there were many.

Finally, after a rather fitful off and on series of dozing in and out, Ben could see the sun coming up over a jagged mountain peak and for the first time realized he was coming into and then out of some of the most beautiful river canyons he had ever seen. This last canyon bottom was surrounded by steep rocky walls on both sides reaching up to higher rocky jagged peaks above pine forests that seemed to stretch forever.

The sun continued to rise as they headed further east and it was now starting to show bright narrow golden rays breaking across the sky as it rose over the top of a nearby mountain range. Man, he thought to himself, "I have seen a lot of sunsets over the ocean back home but nothing like this sunrise, as he watched in awe at the bright colors of sunrise hit the canyon walls and changed the rock formations colors from dark brown to light brown and sometimes almost light gold as the sun rose higher and brighter."

Up ahead, he caught the first glimpse of barns and rooftops. He could plainly see lines of streetlights which were beginning to shut off as the sun was getting brighter and brighter. Not many lights, he thought. Back home in Oceanside, the town lit up like a carnival, but here in this sleepy little town, which resembled something out of a John Wayne movie, the streetlights were few and far between.

The canyon bottom widened as the bus approached Riverton and the canyon walls gave way to wide green fields, divided by fences. The green fertile valley seemed to stretch for miles, and all the pastures were full of horses, cattle, sheep, deer, and antelope. He has never seen so many antelope scurrying around the fields right in the middle of the herds of cattle.

CHAPTER 2

Riverton, at last. As the bus slowed down while entering the town's city limits. Ben could see the local drive-in theater, then a couple sawmills, one with a huge millpond giving way to small pastures or large yards around the houses. It had been 12 hours, two busses, 11 towns, a shit load of weird people; all endured just to travel 350 miles. Travel progress, maybe, but hard on the butt and hardly any sleep.

As the bus pulled into the middle of town, it stopped in front of the local shoe store which doubles as the bus station, Ben looked around for the District Timber Forester he will be working for and who promised he would pick Ben up between 6:00 and 7:00 am and take him up to the work center.

There were two or three people in front of the shoe store/bus stop waiting on the bus and Ben spotted a guy in his 30's. No way this guy fits the bill in his mind of a logger, forester, or woodsman-type.

15

This guy can't be over 5 foot 8, and Ben thought, I am skinny but gawd this guy is the slimmest.

As Ben stepped off the bus, John Parsons, District Timber Forester wandered over to Ben, "Hey since you are the only one under 25 on this bus, I am guessing you must be Ben, my newest crew member for the summer and beyond—am I right?"

Ben looked at this strange little man with his protruding eyeballs guarding an uncommonly large hook nose and sporting a weird stare through what looked like his grandpa's gold horned rim glasses, and that skinny build.

"Yeah, that's me," Ben said, "glad you could pick me up since there is no way I could ever afford to drive clear across the state and keep my truck with me during summer field season and still save any money."

"Hey!" John said, "We are going to stop by the house and have breakfast, Jeane is expecting us and she has made us a quick breakfast before she is off teaching school."

"Great," Ben said as he was thinking about how hungry he was and the fact he sure as heck was not eating anything at the bus change in Centerville. He remembered one passenger yelling at that fat cook waitress that his can of Coke was flat and that his food on the dirty table had too many flies fighting for their share of his sandwich and fries. That was enough for Ben to just leave his order on the table and get the Hell out of there.

They packed up Ben's bag, which was nothing more than his military duffel bag. A bag full of almost everything he owned in the world. They headed over to John's place which was located behind the local food market in a rather nice-sized two-story frame clapboard-sided house.

John, tipped his head up and peered down through his horned-rim glasses starring down at Ben over that hard to not notice large nose, and said, "Not bad for only $65 per month, Heh? I think we got a good deal, most likely because my wife teaches third grade, and I am a Fed with a guaranteed paycheck. In this County, they don't much care for us Forest Resource managers and newcomers, or as the locals refer to us ---'untrustworthy transients' when it comes to managing THEIR local forest."

"But," John added, "we earn good pay, and they know we will not skip paying our bills. Heck, if you weren't born and raised here, the locals don't think you have any business messing with their public lands. However, once they get to know you, you won't have any problems, usually----they just don't seem to like me for some reason."

Ben thought to himself, *he is a little strange, but I wonder why he is so disliked by the locals*, a question that would be answered before the summer field season was over.

John's wife, Jeane, was in the front room as they walked into the rather starkly furnished home. It reminded you of walking into a trailer house, with cheap grooved imitation wood paneling. The paneling had been painted over and every dent and crack showed through the hastily completed paint

17

job. The furniture was plain and worn tan-colored stuff of unknown make. The floor was covered in wall-to-wall light brown thick shag carpet that showed traffic paths like a trail cutting through the forest. Scattered around were a few lamps which provided a minimal amount of light to brighten the place up; and it needed it.

In the corner Ben could see boxes of empty pop bottles along with other jars and bottles and numerous small boxes full of 'stuff'. John had noticed Ben's look of puzzlement and stated "I turn everything into money. I grab and save anything that I find anywhere that has any kind of value or a deposit. If it has value and I find it, it is more money in our bank account."

CHAPTER 3

After a very nice breakfast and lots of good strong coffee, John looked at Ben and said, "Let's head up the mountain. We need to be at the work center by 9:00 am to meet up with some of your new crew members and of course you gotta meet Randy, the camp boss up there. He has been there for the last four years since he started college and the station is pretty much his domain. Just a word to the wise, he can be more than a little ornery and doesn't take any crap from anyone."

****

The ride up the mountain was an eye-opener for Ben, up State Highway 39, alongside Mineral Creek, winding past old, abandoned mining claims with lots of tailing piles everywhere, shacks, and then a few isolated ranch houses. All were strategically built high enough to avoid flooding at the bottom of a narrow canyon. A canyon that supposedly held more gold than anywhere else in the State.

Suddenly, out of nowhere, the road curved around a sharp bend and started up a new canyon, steeper and even more winding, winding beyond Ben's imagination. Switchback curves, one right after another with a maximum driving speed of 15- 25 mph according to the numerous highway warning signs. It wound out before them like a ribbon that had been looped with scissors on top of a gift for the next 10 miles. There were no barriers on the canyon-side of the highway with drop-offs as much as 1,000 feet straight down to the creek bottom below.

When they topped out at the summit, Ben was amazed how quickly the topography became completely flat as they entered a beautiful high elevation valley. There were miles and miles of fertile rangeland surrounded by vast expanses of ponderosa pine forest. Ben thought the whole scene was astounding. Across these high plains, there were grassy mountain meadows broken up small streams and creeks and ringed by dense stands of pine trees as far as the eye could see, stretching clear to the distant horizon.

They turned off the highway down a county road and within minutes, they arrived at the workstation turning sharply off the county road onto a driveway crossing Mineral Creek and then over a cattleguard and into a large parking area in front of what used to be the District Ranger's house back ten to twenty years ago. Now it housed the thinning crew that Ben would be joining.

When Ben stepped out of John's old beater of a pickup, he suddenly knew why this part of the state was so enduring. The very first thing he could feel was the warm late-morning sunlight shining through the tall Ponderosa pines---and wow---those pines. The first thing this boy from the coast realized was that smell, the smell of fresh pine and the feel of the needles underfoot as he jumped out of the truck. He looked up in amazement at the deep blue sky and clouds so white and puffy, he thought he could reach up and touch them. What a change from the rainy and windy coast.

He looked at the house that is now the crew quarters that would be his home for the summer season.

What an impressive old house, Ben thought to himself. It was a tall steep pitched roof styled home with a massive stone front porch with hand-laid stone steps. The entire foundation was also built with the same hand-placed and hand-cut quarry stones. This was typical of the houses from the 1930's built by the Civilian Conservation Corps. There was cedar plank siding around the whole house with massive windows and small pine tree cut-outs were at each end of the house under the eaves near the roof peak and in the shutters on each side of the larger windows.

Behind the crew quarters house were several small cabins, and a little further up the driveway was a small warehouse, gas shack, and around the other side of the compound was a white wooden cage on four legs.

Ben turned to John, "What is that a chicken coop on stilts?"

John chuckled a little and responded, "Actually, that is a weather station. Part of your crew's duties here are to take weather readings twice a day, or more, during fire season. The good news is we do pay you an extra 50 cents per day, but the bad news is someone has to stay here and take the readings on weekends."

This is quite a little compound, Ben thought, *all built in the middle of the forest and miles from anywhere, actually miles from nowhere.* The whole front yard was ringed by a hand-hewn post and pole fence and further out, the compound perimeter was surrounded by a barbed wire fence to keep neighboring ranchers' cattle out of the compound.

The small cabins were particularly nice and Ben soon learned that those were reserved for married crew members or employees doing summer field work. Besides his thinning crew, there was also a crew of fire guards engineers, and along with other summer employees stationed at the work center, such as the married guys. Some of these engineering crewmembers lived in trailer houses at the upper end of the driveway. The center was named 'The Mineral Creek Work Center'. Ben later learned it was named after that creek that flowed about 50 feet away, across the front driveway as they entered the station.

As they entered the front room, Ben noticed it was pretty plainly decorated with an old brown *Herculon* couch and chair and several kitchen type vinyl aluminum chairs lined up against the walls.

As Ben was surveying the inside of the old house, when out of nowhere, Randy entered the room from the hallway left of the living room. "So," he grunted to John, "is this another one of my new girls?"

Ben took one good look at this guy, shuddered, and wondered what in the Hell he had gotten himself into.

There before him stood Randy Thompson, the camp boss of legend, all six foot five inches and 230 pounds of him. He was a hulk of a young man with muscles everywhere, blonde hair, blue eyes, and a menacing almost evil stare. He was a big kid of Norwegian heritage with a rather large head. Above his deep sunken blank-looking eyes was a bulging wide forehead with bones that protruded like someone with a pigeon-chest—he looked like a beat-up pro from Friday Night Wrestling. But in fact, he was in his last year of college in California was a starting forward on their basketball team, sometimes playing backup center. Ben thought, *he could play football anywhere, he must be damned tough under the basket.*

"Come on!" Randy said, "I will show you where you are bunking and where you can put your stuff."

Ben followed him down a short hall to a bedroom with walls of knotty pine tongue and grooved planks. Inside the bedroom were two army-style bunks, one on each side of the room. A small wood table stood by each bed with a small lamp. Outside the bedroom door were two vertical rows of wooden drawers, four high, built into the wall.

"You get the top three drawers on the left," Randy grunted. "The bottom one is mine, stay the hell out of it! Your roommate has already got the same damn message. Unpack your crap and come over to the kitchen and I will show you some of your chores you and the other girls will be doing this summer."

Ben grabbed his Army duffel bag and reached inside, not much inside, three or four pairs of jeans, blue cotton work shirts, a pair of Bermuda shorts, t-shirts and other causal shirts, underwear, socks, and. of course work gear consisting of high-top 8" steel-toed leather boots, wool socks. At the bottom, he pulled out a McDonald Safety-T hard-hat like his dad wore when falling timber, and of course his beat-up leather gloves.

After he settled in, Ben wandered into the kitchen. *Wow*, he thought, *this is more like a kitchen in the restaurant where I worked back home in the summer during college.* On the left was a large gas range with a huge grill over the ovens. There was a huge restaurant-sized fridge located across from large double sinks next to a pantry that could hold enough food for six months. On the other side of the restaurant-style range he could see a gray fifty-gallon government-issue garbage can stand near the back wall.

He turned and looked over by the entry door he just passed through and saw a hand-crank old-fashioned wall phone, powered by two large dry cell batteries. The black metal housing was impressive for such a simple old phone. Ben could not believe anyone still used these old antiques.

Just then Thompson entered the kitchen and noticed Ben staring at the old phone, "You ever seen one of those before? We still have number 9 wire on insulators on trees and poles running throughout the Forest as well as along the roads to all the neighboring ranches. It is the only way we can talk to guard stations, lookouts, and the Forest Supervisor's office. No numbers here he said, we are two longs a short and a long. You get those numbers like Morse code by hand cranking them out!"

Randy added, "I'll tell you the same thing I told the other summer camp girls, stay the Hell away from the phone during lightning storms. It is metal and if lightning is anywhere near the area, it will travel down the lines and ground out through the phone and quite possibly through you!! If you even hear distant thunder, stay off the damn thing!"

Suddenly Ben heard someone yell out, "Hey dude, you must be my roommate," a voice blared from the living room---and into the kitchen walked Wes Jackson, an early arrival at the work center who had been out hiking the hill behind the center. He looked like an evening news clip of a typical war-protesting draft dodger with a full head of long straight black hair, a peace symbol on his t-shirt, and he was wearing a headband with 'Make Love Not War' written across it bordered by white doves.

Ben thought to himself, *Man, I have yet to figure out why I let myself be drafted into the Army and where the Hell was I when I got his personal greetings from the President, in Canada?* Little did Ben know, they would become good friends over the summer, but for now he just wondered what kind of anti-war bullshit he had to endure from his new roommate.

Randy brought things back to reality with, "Listen girls, you are the first at the station, so here's the deal, this my camp, you do what I say! First of all, can either of you cook, oh what the hell probably not? Every day you make your own damn lunches, I cook all the dinners, you girls clear the table, wipe everything down, and do the dishes, and dry and put them away---understood? Now once again, can either of you cook?"

"I cooked breakfasts at a restaurant I worked at during the summers I was in College," Ben offered. "It was mainly for the five to ten night-shift workers, he added, not the general public."

"Did any of them ever get sick---or die, Randy sneered---No?—good, Ben, you and Wes will be cooking breakfasts the entire first week starting day after tomorrow---that's everyone's first Monday morning workday."

CHAPTER 4

Monday morning rolled around quickly for Ben and Wes. Both will be working on the same crew along with several others. The oldest crewmember was named Will Eller. Will was short for William, but he always told everyone, call me Bill!! He lived on ten acres about 10 miles West of Riverton with his wife and four kids.

Randy stated, "You will be meeting another crewmember and self-proclaimed 'greatest crew leader in the world' named Chris Clifton, who stayed in town with some family members. He is from the farming community of Beeton, about 135 miles east near the border. He is just driving up now and he shares the bedroom across the hall from you two."

Ben couldn't help but notice Chris when he first laid eyes on him. My God, I have never seen anyone walk with a swagger like that. He walked straight up, almost backward, swaying slightly from side to side from the waist up and looking slightly down his nose at anyone who entered his comfort zone. Geez, he reminds me of my typing teacher in high school, we used to think she had a stick of dynamite up her butt, she walked so stoically upright.

"So, you guys are part of my new crew, you should be glad you are working with someone as experienced as me," Clifton bellowed.

"You college boys will learn a lot from me. I got to be a crew boss because I learned all this forestry stuff here on the job since I left high school four years ago. You'll get a lot more from me than them books you were cheating out of---this job is more than some damned old sullencutchure college textbook."

"What the hell is he talking about?" Ben asked turning to Wes.

Wes answered, "I think he means silviculture, but hey who knows, what do you expect from someone who has worked for four years in a dead-end crew boss job, man this is going to be an interesting year!"

Ben was only interested in saving money right away so he could bring his truck cross-state and find a place of his own to stay after this year's field season ended. His goals were learning all he could from anyone and everyone and staying out of trouble. He is one of the few people he met so far that wanted to continue this type of work for a career and he knew he had to keep his nose clean, as he already had been promised a permanent position, especially if things went well during this summer field season.

The first week on the job was pretty routine. The crew learned how to determine different areas of the forest that needed to be thinned and then they had to measure the distances around the areas and calculate the acres. Each of these thinning units would eventually end up in a contract to a company or individual hired to thin the forested area to a specified number of trees to remain on each acre.

Bill took Ben aside and said, "Don't worry about Chris, he really means well even if he is in way over his head, he will stand up for his crew."

Bill was an interesting individual. He came from ranching stock and lived within about 20 miles from the family ranch where he grew up. His mom and dad still ran several hundred head of cattle and raised quarter horses and Tennessee Walkers for extra cash. *Beautiful horses,* Ben thought, and they got along very well exchanging stories of Bill's local ranching experiences and Ben's growing up on the Coast, along with his recent tour in Vietnam.

Bill looked the part of a western cowboy, five or six years older than most of the crewmembers, with a sun-weathered face and always with some type of solid silver and gold over-sized rodeo belt buckle helping hold up his well-warn *Levis*. He always wore an old pair of *Levis* which covered the tops of his *Tony Lama* cowboy boots. And of course, on his head, his outfit was topped off by the same sweat-stained old Stetson Bill wore when he arrived at the station for work every day. Bill went home for the weekends, but usually stayed at the work center during the work week. He became a father at age 18 and they had three more in four years.

For some reason Bill did not take a shine to Wes even though the first week seemed to have gone well.

There was just something about the two of them that didn't mix.

****

On Friday, after the first full week of work, the crew drove through Riverton with the intention of letting Bill off west of town before they made their way back to the work center. Bill would come back to the work center by himself Sunday evening. They came into town from the east side of the Forest on their way back up to the Mineral Creek Work Center. The 'rig' the crew rode in was a '65 Dodge 'six pack' a crew rig with four doors and a short pickup bed for equipment. The cab held up to six.

As they stopped in the middle of town, the engine in the '6-pack' made a strange loud grinding noise under the hood and then the motor died but the grinding noise persevered sounding like metal on metal. There they were right in the middle of town at the only four-way stop for fifty miles, which by the way was also the intersection of two state highways.

"Shit," Chris said, "Bill, let's go through our usual routine and you new guys pay attention---Ben get up here and take the driver's seat and grab the key---you start 'er up when I yell to do it."

Like a well-tuned machine Bill and Chris jumped out of the front seat, Ben quickly jumped in the driver's seat behind them.

Bill grabbed a Sandvik out of the back of the truck. Ben had already learned the usefulness of a

Sandvik, which is a two-foot long brush axe with a four inch blade at the end protected by a curved piece of steel—they really were a well-oiled machine as Chris in one motion popped and propped the hood open, Bill jumped up on the bumper and proceeded to swing the Sandvik at the left side of the engine compartment.

The loud grinding noise of the starter motor continued as he kept swinging and striking hard inside the hood whacking the curved metal end of the Sandvik on the Dodge's starter motor. Bill continued swinging that short, handled tool like a sledgehammer pounding the starter motor into submission until somewhere inside its housing something broke loose.

Chris yelled, "Hit the starter Ben!!! and keep 'er cranking."

The starter motor strangely settled down to an oddly sounding yet quieter noise just as the engine started cranking on its own and then with a loud pop and sputter, it finally caught hold and revved up as Ben held in the clutch and pumped the gas.

By now, several locals had gathered near the intersection on the sidewalk, pointing, laughing, and some were even clapping. They always thought the summer 'Feds' those city slickers that invaded their fair cow town were pretty funny anyway, but this was the best entertainment. It was the damnedest Chinese fire drill they had ever seen---once again.

Ben found out this is the fourth time this particular Dodge six-pack had died with the starter motor temporarily freezing up in a grinding mode in the last two weeks. Ben put the truck in neutral and wandered to the backseat while Chris swaggered back to the driver's seat, nodded to the crowd as he replaced Ben behind wheel.

"Boys," --Chris always addressed crewmembers this way---"boys," he said, "I think we beat the hell out of our old record."

Ben was sure the whole process took at least twenty minutes as cars and trucks were starting to line up behind them, probably half the town, but in all actuality this little episode lasted around a minute or two—a record for Chris to brag about.

With the motor running smoothly and Bill dropped off at his house for the weekend, Chris turned the six-pack east and out of town heading back to the work center. Once again, they were on the long drive up that steep winding highway; they travelled at first through open meadows, cool mountain creeks until they got to bottom of 'switchback hell'. This was that ten-mile section of highway that climbed 2,500 feet in elevation those ten miles which contained numerous switchbacks, 1,000-foot drop-offs to the valley floor below, and once again, not one guard rail the whole way to the top. Ben remembered seeing it when he first arrived with John.

CHAPTER 5

Ben, thought to himself, *man I cannot imagine driving this in the winter when it's below zero and there are three-foot snowdrifts.* Chris maneuvered the old Dodge around the first group of tight curves, many which offered scenic vistas of the valley below and the mountains on the other side, truly a beautiful drive, until you meet a logging truck using half of your side. Which they did, as a fast approaching fully-loaded logging truck was barely making the curve ahead of them.

"Damn," Chris exclaimed, "that guy is cutting all these curves a little too close for comfort."

After the logging truck went by and they were about halfway up the mountain, the boys came around one of the sharpest hairpin curves and there sitting at a 90-degree angle blocking half the road was one of the engineering crew rigs, an ugly looking Willys Jeep with its signature looking back end shaped like a box of Nabisco Crackers. These rigs always looked like any slight breeze could tip them over.

The right front wheel somehow had come all the way off and the front axle looked like it was completely detached from underneath and as the front of the Jeep was smunched into a solid wall of granite above the roadside drainage ditch. The entire front end in on the passenger side looked to be caved in a foot or two. The driver and passenger were standing alongside, looking at the mess.

"Hey that's Jay and Walt," Chris yelled, "and Jay looks a little shook up!"

Ben remembered Jay from the earlier Fire Guard School where all the summer crew members went through several days of fire training together.

Jay's eyeballs were as big as saucers and he was shaking slightly. When asked what happened, Jay said, "There was a logging truck coming around the curve up there he pointed, mostly on our side of the road and we either had to go over the canyon edge or cut it hard right into the ditch and the rocks. We chose the ditch and when Walt turned a sharp 90, we pitched over on two tires, came back down on all four and when we did, something up front seemed to snap and then just went sidewise. It felt like the whole front came loose, and we skidded into the ditch and hit that granite overhang on the other side of the ditch."

Chris asked if they wanted a ride to the work center, but Walt declined as he had just radioed the accident to the Forest Supervisor's office downtown. He said they were sending someone out to take some photos and talk to both of them concerning what happened. The County Sheriff was also on his way as they had another driver on this stretch stop at a ranch house and call in a complaint about a speeding 'out of control' logging truck.

"Boys," Chris said, "remember what you just saw, this stretch of road has claimed as many lives as any stretch in the entire state!"

Made a believer out of me Ben thought as they headed back up the narrow winding highway to the work center.

The boys arrived at Mineral Creek and were surprised to see that the newest member of their crew. They all kind of gasped as he quickly jumped up on top of the post and rail fence and then like a gymnast He did a hand-spring on the rails and started walking on his hands, upside down, along the top rail of the fence, never wavering a bit. *Damnedest thing I ever saw* Ben thought, *but damn cool.* He had long bleached-blonde hair and was around six feet tall and well-tanned like he just left the beach. He kind of reminded you of one of those guys in the beach blanket movies.

He hopped off the fence after walking on is hands on the top rail some fifty feet down to the end and bounded back to Ben and the boys like a puppy-dog.

"Hey, I'm Kit from Southern California-----you guys can call me Kahuna, all my friends do," as he offered a handshake to Ben.

"Good to meet you and where did you get a nickname like that?" Ben asked.

"You ever read *Playboy*, there is a cartoon called 'Little Annie Fannie' and one of the main characters is 'The Great Kahuna'. Some of my friends said I reminded them of him since I love the beach and I spend most of my time surfing and chasing girls!"

"Well there you have it," Chris said, "we are almost a total crew, with Kahuna, Ben, Wes, Bill, and of course me, the best damned crew boss in the world. We have one more crew member due to arrive later today or tomorrow, all the way from somewhere back East, Maryland, I think, maybe Baltimore or Virginia, not sure. The plan is to have John bring him up here as soon as he arrives in Riverton on either this afternoon's or tomorrows early morning bus."

"I know none of you have your own wheels, but who owns that old beat up Honda 50?" Chris asked.

Over on the corner of the driveway was this dilapidated red Honda 50 with white trim that looked like it had been tipped over one too many times.

"That's mine," Kahuna blurted out, "I bought it from this guy back in town and John was nice enough to haul it up the mountain in the back of his old jalopy when he brought me up today. I had to spend an extra day at the Supervisor's office to sign some papers and I saw this for sale in the front yard of the house next door."

"I only paid $35 for it; the guy said, *it may be ugly but it runs great and there is nobody left at home here to ride it anymore so it's yours now.*"

Chris retorted, "Looking at this beater, I don't think 'you meet the nicest people on a Honda',

36

applies to your old junker. Definitely not what Honda had in mind in their slogan."

"That is OK," Kahuna replied, "it runs pretty damn well. It goes forever on less than a gallon of gas, I think around 140 miles the guy who sold it to me said. You guys can borrow it if I am not using it on the weekends or even after work!"

Ben thought this might be a cool way to ride around on some of the flatter forest roads in the Blue Hills National Forest and in particular on the Deer Valley Ranger District since that is where the work center was located and there are some really nice forest roads in the area.

Sunday morning was another typical early summer day at the Mineral Creek Ranger Station, with everyone settling in, doing laundry, and oiling up their work boots and getting their work clothes ready for tomorrow morning. Most of the guys had either brought along or bought lunch boxes and a thermos. Most of the lunch boxes were the black barn shaped affairs made of sturdy metal, which was a good thing as stuff gets thrown around quite a bit in their six pack. Chris took his boys around the compound once again and showed them how the gas hand pump worked for filling their Dodge up.

CHAPTER 6

Chris showed them the various types and colors of flagging they would be using to mark their thinning perimeters, and which colors of paint they would be using to mark the trees to either thin or to be left standing. They also got a quick lesson in the care and cleaning of the Nelspot paint guns and the backpack units that held their marking paints.

All this was new to the crew and there were lots to remember and to learn. While they were out and about the compound, no one noticed that John had dropped off the last remaining member of their Timber Stand Improvement or TSI crew as they were called. Chris told them his name is Rob Kurtanz, and that is Kurtanz with a 'Z', pronounced like the word curtains, as they would be constantly reminded throughout the summer.

The boys followed Chris back to the 'cookhouse', as they referred to the old Ranger's house. It really was a cookhouse, because at times other crews joined them for a meal and they all chipped in for the food and of course Randy's list of mandatory chores. They entered the front room of the cookhouse and there on the old beat up couch glancing at the local twice-weekly newspaper sat Rob Kurtanz, that's Kurtanz with a z of course, Ben thought.

He was very smooth skinned, with a fair complexion, narrow eyebrows, and Ben noticed his hands as he held the newspaper. They were very white, with manicured nails, and obviously this guy had never seen a single day of any type of physical work, and Ben doubted he had ever even been outside much. The boys looked at each other thinking, what the Hell have we here. None of them knew anyone who had actually had a real manicure other than perhaps their mothers or sisters and this guy appeared to be more like them than one of the guys---perhaps a little effeminate, Ben thought. Rob was a fairly thin young man, about five foot nine and 145 pounds and he wore khaki pants, a polo style shirt and real fancy all leather sandals. Not the kind of outfit you would see around here.

The guys introduced themselves and even though Rob had probably the limpest handshake in the world, he seem a rather friendly chap, but Ben did notice something very strange and actually a little startling as Rob went back to finishing his newspaper and Ben joined the other's in the kitchen.

"Damnnnn, did you see that?" Ben asked.

Ben rarely swore or said a cuss word out loud, unless he got excited or a little spooked. And he was a little spooked as he told the guys, "You need to really take a good look at Rob's eyes the next time any of you walk in front of or near him. I swear to God. He has the weirdest eyes in the world. One of his eyes was fixed on reading the newspaper and honest to God, the other eye followed me across the entire front room-and he never even moved his head!! You gotta see this for yourself, he stated shakily-- Damndest thing I ever saw."

Later, the boys would learn Rob was from the east coast. He told them his home was about 50 miles north of Baltimore, more or less. But they weren't certain, as Rob was kind of vague about his home and family when questioned.

Wes whispered, "Someone told me that this dude was in some kind of institution or hospital."

And of course, they all quickly jumped to the conclusion it had to be some kind of nut house. Whatever it was, Rob had been recently released and he had been cleared for whatever problems bothered him, mental, physical or whatever. According to Randy, Rob's father was a Congressman or Senator at either the state or federal level and supposedly very influential back east. Rob's father somehow got him assigned to the Blue Hills National Forest for the summer and now will work on the Deer Creek Ranger District with the boys.

Camp boss Randy strolled into the kitchen after Rob went to unpack, and looked at 'his girls' and stated, "You all better watch out for that one. He doesn't look quite right to me and he is as much of a greenhorn as I have ever seen in my four summers here at Mineral Creek. I think he is softer than my pillow and probably about as out of shape as my pillow after a night's sleep. Mark my words, don't let him around anything sharp, hot, or steep without someone watching what the hell he is doing, 'cause he is a walking accident waiting to happen.

Gawd, I swear if you look into his eyes, you might turn to stone. Even Medusa isn't as spooky as he is, you guys better get started on lunches for tomorrow and I will go give the "new sissy-dude" his kitchen and cleaning duties."

****

It was not long after the third week of work with a full crew at the Mineral Creek Ranger Station that Randy gathered his 'girls' into the living room and reminded all of them about that one drawer below their allotted three was his. Now it was time for the explanation.

"Look girls," he said, "there are only two of us in this room old enough to legally drink a beer and just so you know, I make my own. You saw that gray heavy-duty vinyl garbage can with the tightened lid in the kitchen. Don't mess with it or you will be messing with me. It is my latest batch of ale brewing. It should be enough to last me for the rest of the summer. It should see me through another long season and make it a helluva a lot easier to put up with you freaks.

I will be bottling it in the next week or so and those quart bottles will be stored in what used to be your fourth drawer. Don't screw with any of it or you'll be doing the worst camp chores the rest of this summer, got it! I keep a careful count of every last bottle, so consider that this my final warning."

"OK girls," Randy bellowed, "now that we have had you guys and all the other crews working for these past weeks, Monday will be our first monthly safety meeting here at the Work Center. The three district lookouts will be coming down and the engineering crew will be joining us."

Ben learned the district ranger Ned Bash will be attending and will personally kick it off and meet everyone.

Randy added, "He takes safety damn serious so make sure you are on your best behavior and this whole damn house is ship-shape----any questions?"

Randy yelled out, "Hey Kotex," Rob's new nickname, "it's your turn for cooking breakfast, so get your butt up early and be sure and make an extra pot of coffee for the meeting Monday."

Randy and a few others were now referring to Rob as the 'Kotex Kid' or even less affectionately as 'the moron', neither of which pleased Rob. Every time either of those nicknames were used, you could see the feminine features on his face slowly fade and then disappear into a rather bizarre expression of subdued rage, which he couldn't hide and at times scared the Hell out of those around him.

CHAPTER 7

Monthly safety meetings were always a nice way to start the work week as the crews did not have to get up as early on the Monday morning of the meeting. The days at the work center were long. The time clock didn't start until the crews were actually on the job site, no matter how far the drive. This meant if they had to drive an hour to their thinning units, lookouts, or engineering sites, they had to get up at 0500, cook breakfast and clean up. This meant the TSI crew had to make sure all their equipment was loaded and ready to go. They inspected their six-pack to make sure it was road-worthy, loaded up their lunches and personal and work gear and then left the compound about 0645 for an 0800 beginning on their time slip at the job site.

The end of the day was pretty much the same. They all worked until 4:30 pm, loaded up and arrived back at the work center in about an hour, just in time to start dinner. There was no overtime for their type of work and even when a rare opportunity for it happened, it was only straight time, none of that time and a half stuff that the logging and road-building companies paid.

They pretty much had a 10 or an 11 hour day but only received pay for their eight hours of work. Bottom line was that anything that allowed them to sleep in a little extra such as a monthly safety meeting was great for the boys. They also like their weekly 'tail-gate' safety meetings because those occurred in the field and cut down their work time for that day. They were literally held with the tail gate of the six-pack down and crew boss Chris perch on the tailgate like a rooster surveying a henhouse and would lead the discussion on whatever was the safety topic of the week or what safety violations he had seen during the past week or so. He would do this perched on the tailgate while letting his crew know how safety smart he was.

For this particular Mondays' monthly safety meeting, everyone was gathered in the kitchen and living room waiting for Ranger Ned Bash. He arrived about a quarter till eight and Ben and the others stared a little as he walked in as he wasn't what they had envisioned. He was a little man, barely five feet five and couldn't have weighed over 130 pounds.

"Got any coffee," he asked, as his drive up the mountain had taken about an hour and coffee was on his mind the whole way up.

With coffee in hand, Ned kicked off the meeting and discussed some of the same things that had been covered during tail-gate sessions. Proper use of hand tools, no horseplay during work, keeping tools covered with their protective sheaths while walking. He talked about making sure you carried tools on the downside while walking on steep side slopes so you could throw the tool away from you downhill if you slipped, uphill throws might be your last, he explained with little humor. The boys could see he took this whole safety stuff very seriously and actually he was quite interesting and a good speaker and appeared quite fatherly to the crews. When someone asked a question, he responded by finding out their name, what their job was for the summer, and what kind of experience they had out in the woods.

As he concluded the safety meeting, he invited everyone to join him in the kitchen for a final cup of coffee before he returned to town and the boys left for their crew assignments. Ranger Bash poured himself a cup of coffee and promptly popped himself up on top of the gray vinyl garbage can, much to the horror of Randy and 'his girls'. The fact that he only weighed around 130 turned out to be a damned good thing, because he perched on top like he was up in a barber chair and talked to the boys about their summer at Mineral Creek and how things were going, all the time with Randy starting to sweat.

Little did Ranger Bash know he was sitting on 30 gallons of slowly, but quietly bubbling 'Randy' ale.

"Guys", he said, "this place looks really great, you've done a good job keeping it clean and everything is put away where it should be, but something, in this kitchen smells a little moldy or musty. I think you need to really scour out these garbage cans and check the sink drains for clogs. The smell in this kitchen is just a little too much!!"

He hopped off the 30 gallons of ale that could have cost Randy his job and any subsequent references for the future had he fallen through the lid and into the bubbling liquid. Ben thought to himself, man that would have been some sight, imagine seeing our District Ranger fall into a garbage can and take a beer bath while talking safety.

As he walked out the front door, he yelled back at Randy, "It looks like we have a pretty good chance for an early fire season. We have a lightning storm predicted for later this week. Make sure all the tailgate safety sessions cover lightning safety. Talk about what to do in a lightning storm, both out on job and here at the work center."

With that, Wes, Bill, Ben, Kahuna, the Balti-moron, Randy, and the ever-swaggering crew leader Chris headed off to start another work week doing more thinning projects. Wes offered some news to the group that he had completed the needed training to be one of the backup lookouts so the guys and gals up on the district fire towers could enjoy a day off in town. He would spell them once in while working all day Saturday and stay up there Saturday night until they returned from town toward Sunday evening.

"This coming Saturday, I will be up on my first relief assignment on the Slip Mtn Lookout. Ben, if you get bored come up and visit and see the view, I heard it is absolutely spectacular, even for an old hippie like me. Since there is a chance of lightning, that should make things interesting."

Chris, who still was not a fan of Wes offered up, "I am absolutely amazed they would have some long-hair like you up in any lookout watching for fires, especially considering your draft-dodging background.

Wes responded, "That old saying of making love not war is what I believe in and going to 'Nam was never in the cards. Even hippies like me have flat feet, thank Gawd!!!"

CHAPTER 8

After leaving the safety meeting, the boys were still about a 45 minute drive from the job when Wes turned to Ben and asked, "You were in Vietnam until last May, what was it like, did you kill any VC (Viet Cong) or their families?"

Ben didn't respond and remained quiet as this is one topic he had hoped would never come up as all he wanted to do is distance himself from being a draftee and spending time in Vietnam.

"So, Ben," Wes kept pushing, "what the hell was it like, was I right to ride my flat feet all the way to 4F?" (4F was the selective service classification for unfit for service)

"You know Wes," Ben responded smiling, "4F also referred to someone who could have been mentally unfit, you sure it was that end of your body that was unfit, or perhaps the part between your ears, he chuckled loudly?"

"Listen guys, it hasn't been all that long since I got back home, I have hardly spoken to anyone about my tour in 'Nam and for very good reason. Let me give you a little of my background on this, I was there during the Tet Offensive, it was obvious to me as an Intelligence analyst, we had actually caused heavy casualties to the VC all across the country. However, none of this was reported here at home. The only thing in the news at that time and still is, are stories like the massacre at My Lai and the Court Martial of Lt. Calley who is up on charges accused of mass murder. And all this stuff keeps me awake at night. I wasn't out on the front lines, but bad crap can happen to anyone."

"Shit, the way the world is right now, anyone who sees a soldier in uniform or sees a Vietnam returnee, they automatically brands that soldier as a trigger-happy murderer. This may be one of the few times I am going to talk about any of it so let me tell you why I feel this way. I spent a normal length tour plus some extra time in Vietnam after basic training and then going to Army Intelligence school for three months. Yeh, yeh, do not laugh it is not an oxymoron Randy, it was some of the best damn education I have ever been through. I was fortunate to get good grades in college in photogrammetry and that paid off as I was trained amongst other things to become an imagery interpreter in Vietnam.

I was an aerial photo or imagery interpreter of all kinds of stuff like radar, infrared, photos, and I helped prepare tactical terrain studies. That's about all I can really say to you, we all had secret or top-secret security clearances and even though I am done, I can't talk about some stuff. However, we were always told, if your family and friends read about it in the Post, Newsweek, or Times, then we can talk about what went on, but otherwise I can't say much."

"Listen," Ben added, "like I said earlier, I was a noncombatant, and that's another reason I don't talk much about me being there, friends from back home were dying, getting shot up and I had, at least for the first half of my tour, a pretty cushy situation. I worked twelve hours a day six days a week and then a day off and into Saigon or Cholon to see the sights, drink beer, eat good food, and buy stuff for my family back home."

"A few months ago, when my tour ended, and I came home after a long series of flights, lasting 25 hours, I arrived at the bus station downtown near the park in River City. There was a protest going on, some of your buddies Wes, long hair types, you know a bunch of students or wannabe students full of pot and booze, all leading to angry yelling and nasty anti-war protesting with signs being waived by openly stoned or drunk people. So, I got off the bus, and I was in uniform, mainly because we got good airfare and bus rates by travelling that way.

And then a couple of these long hairs come wandering over to me. I am sure they spotted my Vietnam Campaign and service ribbons. They immediately spit at me, called me a baby killer, fascist pig, murderer, you name it-- they yelled it. I got the hell out of there and met my brother and we headed over to the coast to home. I vowed I wouldn't talk about my service again, at least around people that I didn't know well."

The conversation ended just in time as they arrived near the Little Meadow road where they will be starting to lay out some new thinning units.

That day, once again, the crew worked their butts off in the increasing summer heat and after work, on the way back to the work center, the boys continued their question.

"Hey Ben," Chris yelled from behind the wheel, "so did you ever kill anybody??"

"Hell," Ben responded, :we weren't even allowed to have live ammo during guard duty, they kept it locked up. We were an Intelligence Battalion numbering over 1,000 stuck in this tiny old French plantation compound not far outside of Saigon and probably less than two or three acres total in size. All of us supposedly had a small price on our heads, and we had a phony unit name at the front gate so no one would guess what we really were. That part was kind of weird. They didn't want some trigger-happy intelligence dude firing off a live round and drawing attention to us.

So no, I never KILLED anybody---that I saw anyway. But I can say, in my work, we might have been responsible for killing hundreds. Who knows? After all, we plotted targets for B-52 bombing raids as well as napalm drops, agent orange, and other types of shelling's and missions. So, in that instance, we might have killed hundreds in one bombing run, whoever really knew the actual results on the ground?"

"Did you have any close calls," Bill asked?

Ben, thought for a moment and quickly responded, "Yes that's for damn sure, even if you aren't in the infantry, all those months in a war zone usually leads to something happening that affects you and those around you."

"Well I do remember this one time. It was way before the game-changing Tet Offensive that occurred this past February, back when things were still sort of quiet. A couple of us took our Sunday off by going into the city to this restaurant in the Chinese section called Cholon. We went there because we were told by some of our buddies you could get a huge bowl of clams steamed in garlic and white wine, with a huge piece of fresh French bread and a glass of wine or beer all for $1.25.

We decided to have quick beer first at the bar area next door and a couple of the tea girls from the open bar came over and wanted us to buy them a 'Saigon' tea for some sitting down and talking time, which we thought about but decided not to. The three Vietnamese girls sat with us anyone, keeping a wary eye out for their Mama-san, and chatted with us anyway.

All of sudden, out of nowhere, there was this loud explosion. The blast noise appeared to come from just across the street from the direction we had just walked from. As the blast went off, some of the front window glass shattered from the restaurant next door and as we looked up we could see small pieces of wood, glass, and tin being thrown around across the street. Before I could even think, this girl shoved me under the table and to floor and she actually huddled over me under the table until we all figured it was safe. I could not believe she did that without any hesitation whatsoever. And even further, my two buddies said the other girls did the same as all six of us ended up under the table."

"So what the hell happened," Bill asked?

"You know it turned out to be a random thing but damn scary. It was a bicycle bomb. I later learned these things were set off all over the city. In this case we were told the explosives, probably a little chunk of C4 was placed in a loaf of bread that was in a bicycle basket and was parked down a few buildings and across the street.

And the scariest part of this is, the three of us walked right by that bike not 5-10 minutes earlier. We all saw the bicycle and the bread. We didn't think a thing about it, as it was a common sight in Cholon or anywhere in Saigon for that matter.

We did finally have our clams and lots of wine, but we were plenty shook, I can tell you that. But I must tell you those three girls, and in particular the one who pushed me down, that was something I will never forget."

Chris started to say something, and Ben interrupted, "I think that's enough of this, let us talk about something else, ok."

"I'd rather not talk about it anymore right now, maybe someday over a beer as long as you keep things to yourself. As far as you are concerned, if anyone asks about my military service, you don't know a damn thing---ok?"

****

The next morning, after they finally arrived at the thinning unit after getting behind a couple pickup trucks.

Kahuna yelled, "Hey Chris, are all those pickups we saw on the way out here full of hunters, is it deer season?"

"Well, boys," Chris strutted around to the tailgate where they were getting their gear out. "We are in an area where they have allowed a special hunt to help control the overpopulation of mule deer. I think they only have 15 or 20 tags, but this area in and around Little Meadow is the area that has too many deer and can't sustain this heavy population."

"Wow," Kahuna fired back, "you used sustained and population in one sentence, I am damned impressed with all those syllables."

"Just think what you could say if you went back to school," he offered smiling all the way.

The boys were all amused but poor Chris was not---*get to work or I'll make sure Randy gives you girls his dirtiest chores—damn city slickers anyway, smart butts*, he thought.

Since they realized they were now in an active hunting area, the boys tied yellow and red ribbon around their pants legs, on their belts, and onto their hard hats so they were visible to any of the dumb "city hunters" who might accidently put them in their sights. The thinning unit where they were tying boundary ribbons was parallel to the Little Meadow Road. They walked into the thick undergrowth and tied the boundary ribbons along a trail that was only around 10-20 yards from the road at times. The particular unit was thick and overstocked with way too many trees that were three to six inches in diameter; almost too many to walk through and too many to end up as a healthy forest.

This morning, they would mark the boundaries, survey the distance around the unit, and then figure out the acreage contained within the unit. Then, they would put all this on a map and give it a letter or number designation that would be used in the thinning contract.

Once inside these thickets, they needed those colorful ribbons for hunters to see them, dumb city-hunters or not. Chris went ahead of the group and marked the thinning unit by chopping a mark with his cruisers axe followed by the boys using more permanent ribbon to mark the unit as well as them completing the survey to determine the acreage. Ben started tying the yellow ribbon up high every 10-20 feet so the contractor could clearly see the boundaries.

As Ben continued around the corner of the unit heading back toward the road, he heard a gunshot. Hmm, he thought, some hunters must have filled their tag, usually when you hear one just shot out here, it means they were successful.

About a minute later, much to Ben's and everyone else's surprise, they all heard loud gunfire-- bang, bang, bang, and just then Ben heard ping, ping, ker-ping, as he looked down at the ground he could see dust and pine needles flying from a spot where the third or fourth bullet entered the ground just below his right foot, a mere two inches away from a serious gunshot wound.

"Son of Bitch," Ben yelled! "Did you guys see that did you see that someone damn nearly shot my God-damned foot off."

Ben ran full tilt toward Little Meadow Road screaming the entire 20 yards until he got to the road.

The driver obviously heard and saw a half-crazed forest worker running and yelling, as Ben, almost out of breath, watched the hunters beat a hasty retreat down the road away from the crew.

Ben picked up a rock, yelling, "You dumb sons of bitches," and threw it as close to the truck a he could. After throwing the rock in desperation, he hurled every four-letter word he could think of as the pickup sped away.

Get on the God-damned radio and call this in Chris, these guys need some jail time!! Chris responded, "I didn't really see the truck, were they hunting, target shooting, what"?

Exasperated, Ben explained almost out of breath from cursing, "You are not going to believe this."

"There was a guy up front driving and I am damn sure he was drinking a beer, and get this, a guy in the back sitting in an easy chair, a damned easy chair, you know like a recliner, gun on his lap, and he too had a beer in his hand."

"And what happened, Chris asked?"

Ben, slow gather his breath and replied, "I am sure they heard us out there in the brush and start taking 'sound shots' thinking one of us was a deer."

Ben continued, "Damn it, I did not spend all those months in Vietnam only to come home here and have some stupid ass son of a bitch city hunter asshole shoot me or someone next to me, damn those jerks!" Ben turned around to the crew and his cursing stare turned to a slight grin as he said to the crew, "thank gawd they were drinking because I think if they were completely sober, one of us might be hanging in their camp in a deer bag!!!"

Chris, who now realized how close that bullet really came to Ben and the rest of the crew said, "you know boys, I think we have had enough for the day, our last safety meeting was damn good, but this afternoon tops anything I could think of to discuss!!! Let us go home, even if it is an hour early, we have damn sure earned it.

CHAPTER 9

lthough, lightning across the Blue Hills National Forest was not a big deal, none-the-less, everyone took it quite seriously, not only from a work safety aspect, but of course the worse-case scenario, a forest fire. The mountain country of the Blue Hills National Forest was one of the top ten places in the world for recorded lightning strikes. Tuesday evening after dinner, the boys talked about the upcoming possibility of a lightning storm and whether there would be any fires.

Camp boss, Randy stepped in and reminded them, "Look you guys are not a regular fire crew but you have all been trained to do the initial attack on small lightning fires, so you damn well better be ready. You could go out as a two or three-person lightning fire attack group. We also need to get this place storm-ready. I need to have you guys make sure all the Coleman lanterns are full and the mantles are in good shape, because when the storms hit, we always lose our electricity and will need the lanterns."

Kahuna, Ben, Wes, you three go through all the lanterns, check them out, and test them. Kotex, you watch and learn, but don't touch, you hear me?"

Rob's hate-filled stare at Randy fully displayed to everyone his response as he boiled under his breath and outward demeanor. Randy missed it, but the boys saw the rage!

On the front porch, Ben went through the entire supply and made sure all the mantles were ok and that the pumps worked fine and each of the lanterns were all fueled up. He had used these many times when the power went off during the numerous coastal storm back home. Ben went back inside after he finished. In the meantime, no one noticed Rob sneak out on the porch. He decided he would go ahead and check the lanterns since he didn't see anyone else around. In his infinite wisdom, he decided he knew exactly how to check things out, how to clean the lanterns, check the mantles, and fire up each Coleman he was looking at without any help from his detractors. *Crap*, he thought to himself, *I'm not an east coast greenhorn, I have camped----well camped in a cabin, anyway, well ok a summer home he reminded himself.*

Rob grabbed a lantern as he sat on the front porch and did the appropriate burning off the mantle and he knew the fuel level was fine. He then pumped the hell out of the lantern with the short little hand pump on the side. *Shit*, he said to himself, the tank was not sealed tight enough as some of the kerosene spit out onto his jeans and onto the porch. He tightened everything up, re-pumped at least 30 more times and decided things were OK. He grabbed a Diamond stick match and quickly struck it and place the match flame inside the glass, under the lantern mantle and with the glass lifted, flames from the mantle whooshed loudly and swiftly as flames licked like a huge tongue from under the glass causing the kerosene on Rob's pants to instantly catch fire and spread across the continuous spill on the concrete front porch.

Ben heard the cry and ran out the front door and to his instant horror, saw Rob on fire on both pantlegs burning from the knees down. As Rob screamed for help and Ben yelled for someone to bring the first aid kit. He quickly pulled off his sweatshirt and snuffed out the flames before they could spread or cause a serious burn.

"You dumb son of a bitch! Ben exclaimed, "What the hell were you doing?"

Randy ran out with the crew behind him to see if an ambulance was needed. The Kotex kid looked up and sheepishly stated, "I knew what I was doing, this damn lantern is screwed up and Randy, why the hell is it even in service, you are the supposed to be the big king of the camp-what's with you dumbo?"

They all looked at his smoking pants and the scorched area on the porch, and Ben finally asked, "how the hell many pumps did you do to that lantern. Oh, 20-30 the first time, then with the mantle readied, another 20 or 30 times," Ben said, "you are so damn lucky, you put so damn much pressure in that lantern, plus you didn't bother to clean up the spilled kerosene on your clothes and on the porch, you could have blown up the whole area." "You may not think much of our camp boss, but he knows these lanterns and no one has ever had a problem until you didn't listen and damn near pumped your butt into self-destruction."

Are you that stupid? From now on, you listen to what you are told, or else you are heading back home---got it?" "Listen" Ben stated, what you and the others need to understand here is, "I am in this job for a long-term career, you are here for some kind of western movie adventure. I think by now you understand, out here, this is all for real, not some move script. You scared the hell out of all of us, as we all look out for each other, but you better start damn well start looking out for yourself!!"

Everyone went back inside as the reality of an approaching workday morning and another long day in the woods would soon be upon them. Even though it was only 7 pm and considering the idiot hunters along with the idiot easterner almost burning his legs off, it was a tiring day for all.

With the week's work winding down, Bill reminded the crew to be "lightning-careful" as he got ready to go home for weekend. "I have seen plenty of close calls with lightning storms even near my place at the lower elevations down in the valley." As he continued his warning, he looked out the window of the six-pack and noticed a small black plume of smoke off in the distance. "Damn, he commented, look at that smoke, no storms yet, I wonder where the smoke is coming from?"

"I gotta sneaking' feeling I know what that is all about Chris stated emphatically," as if he actually knew something. "Once in a while, the District honchoes will have one of our old, abandoned cabins burned down, or an old line-shack. What I hear is they are purposely burning down all the old, abandoned sheds, barns, corrals, and cabins that they cannot make safe for the public, usually when no one is watching."

Not sure if this 100% true, but what I heard was, someone somewhere, like in Colorado, either a mom or dad or their kid were snooping around an old mining cabin and then all sudden one or all of them fell into an old mine shaft. This kid, according to what I heard, died, I think that's the story, I don't know, anyway. Since there ain't no way to make these places safe and there are so many, District folks are just burning them down, filling in shafts when they find them and bulldozing these places over. Same thing, here, this is not the first one of these fires Bill and I know about. I am sure more will be burned and who knows how many have already burned. I know it's all rumor, but I remember hearing from some of the old-timers down in the Supervisor's Office saying that they did the same damn thing to abandoned cabins way back in the 30's, so who knows!! It sure as heck wasn't a lightning strike."

CHAPTER 10

"**H**ey, you guys, wanna hear something funny," Chris asked. "You all met John, right, our District Forester. Now you guys all need to remember even though we hardly ever see him, he is our immediate overall boss and we do in the long run work for him. After all, he does head up all the timber programs including our thinning work. Anyway, from what I have heard, he gets way too carried away when it comes to enforcing contracts. He does not trust any of the contractors who do thinning on the units we work on. I am not sure why, but he is definitely a strange guy and I have been working with him for three years now."

"You guys know we are going to change our methods of contracting out the thinning stuff; we are going to go from marking every tree with blue paint that needs cutting to writing a "choppers choice" contract where we tell the contractors what we need them to leave and at what spacing. They cut the rest on their own. John hates this idea and is fighting it so he sneaks out on weekends to watch ongoing trials of this new thinning work to see if they are screwing up."

"So, the story I heard was that he snuck out to spy on a contractor near here last weekend. He was supposedly on a picnic with his wife and family. But when they were out near a contract site, he left them down along the road to pick up bottles, cans, and any other kind of prized junk he collects. Meanwhile, while they were doing his scavenging, he crept through the woods and hid on a little hill behind an old log where he could see the thinners, but they couldn't see him, so he thought. He stayed there quietly watching the contractor's thinning crews working down below him for quite some time. They were pretty much cutting down everything exactly as we marked it for them or if their choice, they were making the choice to cut or leave correctly. Nothing really going on out of the ordinary. As he spied from his perch stretched out behind that big old log, Old Windy Johnson, the contractor, had spotted a flash of sunlight coming off of John's horned-rim glasses from where he was hiding up on the hill."

"Old Windy decided to leave his crew and do a little sneaking around on his own. Can you guys picture this? So, imagine this, old Windy guy creeps way up around the backside of the hill where John thinks he is safely spying from and just when John is settled in; all of sudden up behind him comes Windy."

"John hasn't seen him nor does he have a clue that Windy, who is getting on in years, is right behind him using a shovel handle as a walking stick. Because of the sound of the chainsaws, clueless John does not suspect that Windy is just a few feet away from where is sprawled out behind the log, spying."

Windy got close and took the shovel handle in both hands like a baseball bat and swung it quite hard. Whack----right across John's butt goes the shovel almost as hard as he could swing, at his age. John, startled, like he had been attacked by a crazed nut case, yells every profanity he can think of at a laughing Windy and John then beat a hasty retreat as fast as he could back down to the road grabbing his butt the whole way. He quickly ended up down on the road where his wife and kids were still looking for his favorite trash. They were all puzzled at the sight of their dad and husband running down the hill toward them, cursing out loud, holding his butt and muttering more swear words as he approached them. His face was as red as the town's fire engine.

"After the shovel whacking, Windy made sure he spread the story around town, that's how I heard about it," Chris added. From what I heard, the guys in the office left a pink girlie-looking whoopee cushion on John's desk chair the next Monday morning with a "hope your butt gets well" card attached.

Considering the week's events, this is exactly what the boys needed to hear and the laughter continued all the way back to Mineral Creek. *Funny stuff,* Ben thought, sometimes true stories are way more weird than anyone could dream up. The boys got back to the work center and unloaded all their equipment with an upward glance as anvil-shaped clouds were forming off in the distance to the southwest.

"Looks like a pretty good build-up starting to form for a thunderstorm Saturday or Sunday, Chris warned. We may not be a fire crew, but remember what Randy said earlier, we can be sent out on initial attack on small lightning fires anytime of the day or night. So, make sure all the tools are sharpened and ready."

As happened every Friday evening after work, they decided who was going to stay at the work center and take the weather readings twice a day over the weekend, and the others were free to do their laundry, grocery shopping, or just head to town for some fun.

Just then, a car pulled up to the cattle guard in the driveway and honked. Everyone could see the two cute girls in the car, giggling and laughing and honking their horn. They were both decked out in tight cut-off jeans and a tight top.

"Who the heck is that?" yelled Wes.

Kahuna looked at the car, and then with a huge smile on his face and beamed, "That's my ride into town for the weekend. I will see you guys Sunday evening, should be a damn fine time in town boys!! Sorry you can't join me, well actually no I'm not," he laughed. "Ben, here's the key to the Honda; you can go ahead and ride it over the weekend, it's got a full tank in her. Just don't wreck it," he laughed, knowing it was his "gutless wonder" on two wheels; it could barely hit 40 mph downhill.

Ben thought, *Cool, In between weather readings, I'll drive around the local County roads and head onto some of the easier Forest roads.*

CHAPTER 11

"**B**en," Wes called out, "I am heading to be up on Slip Mtn. Lookout this weekend as the backup. I will be going up bright and early tomorrow morning and coming down from relief duty Sunday night. Why don't you make a sandwich or something and come up and see the lookout later tomorrow and have a little lunch? It is the closest lookout to the work center and since you have Kahuna's 50, it should be an easy ride. I don't think it is more than six miles total from here, you just take the County road back toward town and take the first left; there is a sign there with the mileage to the lookout."

That got Ben really excited as he was really looking forward to exploring a little on the old Honda and it seemed like Saturday morning would take forever to arrive. Ben looked outside and noticed those large thunderheads developing weren't so much anvil shaped anymore and now were building up high into the atmosphere, a good indication of lightning coming. The LAL (lightning activity level) for tomorrow was predicted at an LAL3. That means a pretty good chance for lightning. It could be an interesting day to visit Wes up on Slip Mtn., Ben thought.

Ben, Chris, Rob and a couple guys from the engineering crew were told to stick around in case of fires, and they enjoyed a cooler Friday evening playing poker and telling dumb jokes, as the cloud-cover kept the temperature down and the humidity was quite a bit higher. "Feels strange," Ben stated, "kind of smells like rain. Chris, you know this country, what do you think."

Chris strutted around the room in his usual display of self-importance, like some rooster on a vitamin overdose, "Yeah, thunderstorms tomorrow. Perhaps settling in across the whole ranger district; you better plug your ears Kotex, cause your mommy ain't out here from Merryland to protect you," Chris said with a huge grin.

Chris never did like easterners; actually, Chris wasn't overly fond of anybody that wasn't from farming or ranching country.

Rob fired back to Chris, "You ignorant beet farmer, quit calling me Kotex, use my damn name or you are going to be sorry as Hell."

"Shit," Chris said, "I am sorry now, sorry you are such a damn greenhorn, Baltimoron. You damned near burned your legs off, set the porch on fire all because you didn't listen, and you are so damn dumb about outdoor ways." What the hell did you do outdoors when you were younger, play with your sisters? So, Kotex, just shut up and do what the Hell you are told; you are starting to irritate me more than a little." Chris sauntered over to the chair next to the old couch and leaned back a little against the wall.

Rob leapt to his feet, his smooth feminine facial features had now turned into a distorted and twisted angry face. His eyes were squinting and the veins in his neck were popping out as he turned red, yelling, "Chris you son of a bitch, don't fuck with me anymore and never call me Kotex again or call me a moron" as he jumped over on Chris and clenched both hands in a tight choke-hold around Chris's neck. He pushed Chris back further into the chair against the wall and tightened his grip.

"Let go of me you crazy bastard," Chris yelled. "Get him the hell off of me you guys."

Ben and Wes ran over and tried to pull Rob off Chris by grabbing his wrists and tried to pry his fingers loose from Chris's neck.

"I can't free his hands," Ben yelled.

"I can," Joe one of the engineers exclaimed as he grabbed a small chair in both hands, swung it like a baseball bat and caught Rob right in the ribcage causing him to loosen his grip, as the rest of the engineering boys jumped in and restrained the enraged and still very mad Rob.

Rob looked back at Chris with a continued distorted and sinister smile, and said "What's a matter Chris, did you think this little sissy easterner was going to hurt you; don't worry if I wanted to, I would have. That was just a warning and that goes to the rest of you too, don't mess with me or I will defend myself anyway I can." Rob seemed to make believers out of everyone at the work center that he could take care of himself. But the way he did it also indicated he most assuredly was some kind of mental case as no one they knew settled arguments or teasing by choking the hell out of someone.

Everyone settled back down as Chris mumbled a muted "sorry" about the teasing, "even if your sissy-ass deserved it." Chris added that last part to make sure he ended up on top of the situation, at least in his mind.

As they started playing another game of blackjack, Chris tried to change the whole atmosphere in the room as he asked Ben, when you were in Vietnam, "what's the weirdest thing you can remember." Ben kind of scowled at the question but then thought for a minute for an appropriate answer. With a slight grin on his face, he replied, "you know, one of the damndest thing I remember was watching a fish walk right out of the damn river right up toward where I was standing."

Ben decided to answer the question since there was so much tension in the room. "We had a club on the compound where we could drink beer, play cards, watch live shows. The shows were mostly Filipino bands that imitated popular bands from around the world. Some were quite good and some were quite bad; anyway, one night I remember watching the band for a while, had a few beers, maybe a few too many beers, and then I walked back toward my barracks which was the building closest to the Saigon River and since the monsoon rains had started, the river was up quite high, and had started to run into our walkways.

I looked down under the lights, and there was this damn fish, and it was walking toward me, across the bank above the swollen river. It was standing on what looked like two front legs with the back part resting on his tail. He just kind of wiggled back and forth on the leggy looking things up front and pushed with the tail, I guess. Damn, it was a big one, over a foot long and probably weighed a pound. I found out from guys who had been there a while it was a SE Asian Walking Catfish."

The boys listened intently, and one of the engineer guys said, "I find that a little like bullshit, I have never seen a fish with legs." Ben offered, hey, "you don't have to believe me, go look in the Encyclopedia Britannica, it has a great story about those types of fish. I had to go back and look it up myself just to make sure it wasn't the beer clouding my memory." Ben was in a talking mood, unlike most times when it came to questions about his service.

One of guys asked, "what did the country actually look like, Saigon, for instance, all we see on TV is dead people, jungle, planes dropping bombs, and all we hear on the news is how we should win the war right away as they talk about numbers of dead Viet Cong."

Ben thought about all those questions and as much as he hated to talk about his relatively easy time in Vietnam, as he called it, he did respond. "Look, he said, the people there are amazing. They have these ugly old yellow and blue taxi cabs that I swear were left over from the late 40's, but they keep them running with wire, tape, chewing gum and god knows what else. The whole country was actually left with a pretty good infrastructure from the French. I saw maps of parks, there were sewer systems in place, water systems, and of course roads and bridges. People were friendly to me and I never had someone threaten me while walking in the city. Of course, that is when we actually could go into the city on our day off.

Saigon had city parks, a university, a wonderful zoo, botanical gardens, a golf course, and the city itself was relatively safe until the Tet offensive attacks. What I remember most, is how stifling hot it was when I got off the plane at Ton Son Nhut airbase. When you first got there, it literally hit you like blast furnace blowing through a hot wet shower. Listen, when I got up in the morning in the barracks and polished my boots, sweat just ran down my butt like a river, I could not believe I would ever get used to the weather, but –we did. And all in all the whole area that had not been touched by the war consisted of a beautiful old French city with lots to see and do. Wes asked Ben, "now that you are home along with so many others, don't you think it will be over by the end of summer, we should really kick the Viet Cong and

North Vietnamese the hell out of there by then, right"?

Ben thought for a minute and answered, "No, it's pretty clear to me with all the war hippies protesting and getting all the news coverage around the world and people here sick and tired of seeing so many kids our age getting killed, I think it's pretty much over for us. And then you have the likes of Hanoi Jane with some people accusing her of committing treason. We are too moral to win war. Look, all we had to do was bomb the dikes along the rivers by the cities of Haiphong and Hanoi, but since that would be an immoral act against the civilian population, we shied away from it. There are dikes along the Red River protecting numerous industrial sites and facilities, we could have bombed those and flooded their entire industrial complex during the monsoon season and that could have helped end the war immediately. But of course, we would have killed thousands of civilians, once again, we were too moral politically speaking."

Let me tell you how I learned about how hard this war would be, even if I was in an Intelligence unit and had access to all kinds of information that you guys wouldn't believe, I still wondered why we hadn't won already. When I got to Vietnam, I never considered myself naïve, but from news reports, I also thought we should be kicking butts and going home quickly.

I asked with one of the Lieutenants in our group, shouldn't we have this over and done with before my tour is up? "We have superior everything from what

I can see." That Lieutenant said, "hey listen, I thought the same thing, but I found out things are never as they appear. Here," he handed me a book and said, "read this book. It absolutely changed how I thought about this war and how I looked at things from then on. The book was titled *Hell in a Very Small Place.-The Seige of Dien Bien Phu.*"

"What the hell did that mean," Chris asked in his usual blustery manner, "a bunch of commie pinko written crap so we would leave in defeat"? Ben replied, "No listen, in the 50's the French were cornered at this place up north and even though they were superior in every area of war, weapons, technology, military training, equipment, and of course money, they could not figure out one thing.

That thing was the resolve of a people with less of everything. This sometimes means protecting what they thought was their heritage, their history, their country, and it is stronger than any war machine. Listen, what they had was hundreds, and at times even thousands of their countrymen walk hundreds of kilometers south down those jungle trails and then pick up a howitzer round or other munitions or supplies, whatever each could carry, turn right around and carry the load on their back and the trek hundreds of kilometers back up North to help their General Giap and the Viet Minh who had the French surrounded. "

****

80

Each of them would make the grueling trip, drop off the howitzer round or whatever they were carrying, and then guess what they would do next Chris?' Chris said, "probably go have a beer or that gross sake shit, and see the family"?

"Not at all," Ben added "after a short rest, they headed back down the trail the hundreds of kilometers and picked whatever else was needed, and start the trip north all over again to resupply the Viet Minh who finally ended up defeating the superior French forces, forcing their surrender."

"What is really funny," Ben added, "was the bus driver that drove us every day from our compound SE of Saigon over to the Intelligence Center was a member of the Viet Minh forces who helped defeat the French. He told us the funniest stories imaginable, a new one on every bus ride it seemed. He spoke great English, Vietnamese, and of course he was fluent in French. He thought the French were too self-assured and proper to win the war and that perhaps we Americans were too rich and too improper to lose, boy was he wrong."

"Listen guys," Ben stated tiredly, "it's getting late and I'm not much on war stories but you know it's just how I see things. We are too moral to do the things we need to do; we don't have the will to kill thousands of civilians where TV can cover the story, but we can sure as hell kill them one on one for a body count. I remember reading casualty reports about kills from different units. The reports would state, a name suspected VC age 12, or suspected VC age 9, or suspected VC age 83, or, well you get the picture, we looked at things like it was a scorekeeping exercise and dead bodies were our wins. But, hell, what do I know I am just guessing, I think that's probably all I should say about my opinions, you never know who is listening out there to people like me who were in a unit like mine. I am heading to bed, Ben finally said---listen---some other time, maybe, more about things I experienced in 'Nam but not any more tonight, see you guys in the morning.

"Kotex, you damn well better cool it, we all have nicknames we didn't ask for, but here in this camp, that is how we are, get over it!"

CHAPTER 12

The morning's weather looked like the prediction from earlier in the week was right on the money. Lightning was definitely on the way, as the morning buildup of clouds was already beginning to look dark gray, ominous and threatening. Ben made a quick lunch of a sandwich and some chips and stuck it in the little saddle bag of the beat up ugly old Honda as he got ready to ride up to the lookout and see how Wes was doing in relief of the full-time lookout. He told everyone he was leaving and if needed they could radio him via Wes at the lookout.

Ben rode out the driveway and carefully crossed over the cattleguard, chattering every bone in body as well as jarring every loose part of the old bike. He hoped the damn thing would hold together. He turned out onto the paved County road where the little bike actually was quieter with a smoother ride. He only had to go a couple miles toward the turn off to the lookout. The old bike did start out fairly quiet and then suddenly it sounded like a lawnmower engine with no muffler, way too loud, rattly, and of course, gutless. But he did get it up to 35 mph on the flat paved road. After a couple miles and many minutes, he turned left onto the road to the lookout. It was after this turn, that the pavement turned into gravel as he headed onto the three mile-long uphill run to the Slip Mtn. Lookout. Slip Mtn. Lookout is one of the nicest lookouts in the West with fantastic views of two valley floors below. It is around 6,500 feet I elevation and provides far-reaching views of the forest 360 degrees around it, making a great fire lookout.

The old bike was doing damn good Ben thought as he started up the very last part which of course was the steeper section. All of sudden, the motor on the bike started wind down, his speed went from 30 to 20, to 15, down to 10. The little bike grinded its way up hill another hundred yards and slowed down to no movement whatsoever. Shit Ben thought, a half a mile away and the hill is too steep to for the little bike to carry me and the weight of this old rattle-trap up the hill.

Ben decided the only way make that last half-mile was to get off the bike and walk alongside it is giving it whatever throttle it needed to move it up the hill, riderless. It only took him another 30 minutes to get to Slip Mtn. But it was worth it as Ben looked around and marveled at the views in all directions. The lookout rose above him some 80 feet above ground. He looked up at the tiny little cabin perched on top the erector set looking structure accessed by several flights of metal stairs. At the bottom of the lookout was an outhouse, a small storage building, and a single tower with several sets of antennae pointing toward Riverton, some 10 miles below in a straight line.

You could see Riverton way down below at the end of the long beautiful green valley and well to left. Almost 180 degrees West was another high-country valley that he assumed was the same as where the Mineral Creek work center was located. He yelled up at Wes letting him know he had arrived. It only took about an hour despite the last bit of walking and pushing and cajoling the old 50 that last half mile. Wes yelled down to bring up the water in the stainless-steel milk can that was at the bottom of the stairs.

That's just friggin wonderful, Ben thought, *now I gotta lug 50 pounds of water all the way up those four flights of stairs that snaked back and forth up the middle of the lookout's support structure. Not a problem,* he thought, until he hit the last section and remembered, *damn, I forgot we were at the 6,500-foot elevation.* That's almost 1,500 feet higher than the work center, and it really started to wear on him, but he finally made it up to the small cabin perched on what appeared to be four rather unassuming supports. It had a catwalk style balcony about three feet wide with metal railings around the whole cabin and one entry door on east side.

Inside, Wes thanked him for binging up the water. "We were almost out, and I can't leave for a break unless someone is here to monitor the radio and telephone or one of the other lookouts can see this direction," he said.

"Cool man!!, You have a real honest to gawd telephone, up here, hell bells and we still have those old crank telephone machines, I can't believe it," Ben exclaimed.

Wes, keeping his eyes on the horizon answered, "this is one of the few lookouts in the West that actually has electricity; if you look down to the west you will see a power line that goes to all the ranches and the work center and also a new telephone line that is following the power line through the forest. That goes right by here, see, just over there a hundred yards."

I heard that by the end of this summer, crews will take down all the Number 9 wire as new lines and new up to date telephones will be installed at all the outlying ranches as well as at the work center. No more dry-cell operated lightning rods in our lookouts, guard stations, or crew quarters.

"What's the deal with the insulators on the bottom of the legs of the stools, table, and the fire finder table," Ben asked.

"Those old insulators that are screwed into all legs that touch the floor are our safety net. When lightning gets close enough to hear, you better pop up on the stool, keep your feet off the floor and you sure as hell better keep from touching anything metal, and wait out the storm, Wes commented as if he had been here for years. Otherwise, we could end up toast or worse. I have been told that one lookout had to stay put for six hours, no food, no water, and no peeing." Wes added "look at my cot, it also has insulators attached to the legs, so at least I can sit out the storms in comfort if they hit while I am here."

"Remember, the lightning can shock the hell out of you if you touch anything metal. I can't even use the fire finder until after the storm has passed. But," Wes stated, "you actually can't spot any fires until the storm clouds clear anyway. Notice what's in the corner."

"Wow, I can't believe you have a tv up here, can you really get a picture up here,?" Ben asked, excitedly as he spied the tiny set.

"At this elevation and being about the only lookout with electricity, the TV actually can pick up a couple channels via repeaters, snowy, but still watchable," Wes answered.

Wes and Ben dove into their lunches as they both kept a watchful on the lightning storm as it was rolling in from the Southwest at a very fast clip. As they finished their lunch, huge dark gray cumulous clouds formed straight overhead with rising dark black tops. They both took a walk around the lookout cabin on the walkway, and Ben was the first to spot a lightning strike about three miles away, across the canyon.

"Damn, Ben, look at that storm moving our way and damn fast," Wes said, "it will probably hit us within a half hour, so we need to get everything in off the catwalk that could blow away. The wind gets pretty strong up here during lightning storms, even small ones, as high as 50-70 mph I have been told,"

They quickly secured everything, including the windows that were all swung open on all four sides, securing them with the several latches on each window. They closed the door and bolted it in and prepared for the oncoming storm.

Fifteen minutes later, thunder started booming across the distant valley and could be heard all the way up to the lookout and it was getting jet engine loud. A few minutes later, Ben saw the next flash and it was only about a mile away as he counted around seven seconds from when he spotted it until when he heard it.

"It's heading right toward us Wes; do we have to get on the stools?"

"Damn rights, we sure as hell don't want to wait any longer, because a mile is damn close, and it could hit the lookout next time," West answered. "We do have lightning rods and the whole lookout is grounded, however, we aren't necessarily safe from getting shocked at any time if we touch metal, like the stove, heater, fire finder."

It started to get dark as the sun was completely blocked by thick black clouds and visibility was down to a half mile. Lightning could now be seen streaking across what limited sky was available, and cloud lightning glowed through all the surrounding clouds.

"It was truly a beautiful but scary sight," Ben thought to himself; *"damn this is so cool."*

Bright flashes were now coming from several locations, and the thunder was now almost instantaneous and deafening at times, meaning the lightning was within a quarter mile. The two of them perched on their stools, glass insulators firmly attached to the legs and the floor as they surveyed what little they could see out any of the windows.

****

Ben was momentarily lost in thought. He seemed to be having more and more memories of his Vietnam tour. They weren't necessarily nightmares, but just memories of things that happened. His mind now quickly flashed back to the night of the Tet Offensive in Vietnam. The VC and North Vietnamese regulars were staging nation-wide attacks on dozens of major US and South Vietnamese installations across the entire country.

The memory became more and more vivid, there he was at the Intelligence Center near the airbase in the safety of a building with no windows and a roof and wall system designed to withstand direct hits from 220 mm rockets and smaller mortars. But that didn't matter as officers in command that night told everyone.

"Look we have several roof access hatches where some of you will be going up on top and guarding this compound against attack. Sandbags are set up in an L-shape at each corner of the building and you will go up for guard-duty until ordered to stand down."

"Ben, you are up with Sgt. Williams and Spec Inswell on the SW corner. Get your weapon and ammo and go down to the corner of the building and climb up through the hatch."

After climbing up on the roof, Ben thought, "*Shit, what the hell now??*

Sgt. Williams looked at Inswell and Ben and said, "Look, odds are we are all just going to be fine, the airbase is several hundred meters away, the Joint General Staff Compound is to your left another 200 meters, and the South Vietnamese HQ is right next door to them. Those are the main targets of possibility. We are just here, a small unassuming support building, at least that is what we have always wanted the enemy to think. No one really knows there are 700 of us inside doing intelligence work." You are absolutely not to fire unless I give you the order to shoot."

Ben's eyes opened a little wider as he snapped back into the present. Wes looked over at him and asked, "are you all right, you look a little unsettled. We are perfectly safe here?"

"No, I am fine, Ben answered, sometimes I just keep remembering or thinking about things that happened in Vietnam, some good some bad."

****

Crack, boom!!! The noise echoed throughout the cabin as it was lit up by a nearby lightning strike which filled the whole lookout cabin with a bright white light. As Ben continued to snap out of his daydream, rubbing his eyes as he looked over at the fire finder.

He absolutely could not believe what he saw as dozens of tiny little balls of white and yellow electricity rolled around the top. Then, suddenly, he noticed more of the miniature fireballs rolling over the top of the metal cook stove and they were bouncing like jumping beans and then just as quickly as they appeared, they all disappeared.

Ben yelled to Wes, "did you see that have you ever seen anything like that in your life--so damn cool? I cannot believe we just watched little balls of white electricity roll around the lookout. Is that what they call St. Elmo's fire?"

Whamm!!! another lightning strike hit close to the lookout causing the whole support structure to shake followed by then another huge strike which crashed by the lookout striking a granite outcrop some 200 feet straight down below the lookout. Ben watched it hit and then he saw one of the most amazing examples of nature imaginable, something he may never see again in a lifetime. A yellow-orange ball of lightning the size of shape of large basketball literally bounced off the side of the granite and bounced to the ground and rolled a few yard downhill, and then it disappeared. Ben just stared at the granite outcrop in disbelief, shaking his head. The storm continued and was now about as intense as he had ever witnessed.

Lightning began to flash everywhere and the thunder roared like an out of control freight train with accompanying winds lashing out against the four walls of windows.

"Stay up on that stool right now yelled Wes," as another bolt of lightning hit close by and once again everything inside rattled from the thunderous noise of the storm. Ben thought to himself, *I hope these damn windows are strong because that is all there is between us getting blown off this friggin overgrown power pole.*

A few minutes later, as quick as it started, the lightning storm began to subside and the thunder started to slowly fade away. You could now count over fifteen seconds between the flash and the thunder meaning two miles to the strike and heading away from the lookout, but now moving toward the Mineral Creek Work Center.

"I better get back to the work center, "Ben stated. "Some of those ground strikes were damn close to there and I think all of us will probably be sent out."

"Except Kahuna, of course, he will be having a little fire of his own to deal with," Wes stated, giggling like a little schoolgirl.

CHAPTER 13

Ben hopped on Kahuna's rusty trusty Honda 50 and headed back downhill to the work center. Since this was a downhill ride almost all the way, he made the return trip twice as fast, and a hell of lot easier he thought. As he bumped across the cattle guard and entered the compound, he could see a bunch of activity with some of the engineering crew loading their pickups. Bill was back from town early and getting tools and water loaded and Rob was actually busy filling the large orange canteens and canvas water bags.

"Hey dipstick," Randy bellowed. You better go get into your work clothes and get your gear ready to go. We're all going to be dispatched out chasing smokes this afternoon and tonight." "We have had dozens of ground-strikes on the district and its all hands on deck, even if you are all a bunch of sissy hands, there's still going to be a fire for everyone." Just then, Randy heard the phone ring and he ran in to take call. After about five minutes he came out and relayed, "Ok, here is the deal," and he handed out locations of known fires and areas of multiple strikes with assignments to everyone. After he was finished, he looked over at Ben and said, "you and I are staying behind, there was a smoke report around a half-mile on that hill just behind the work center, but now it's laid down and the lookouts will crosscheck the location the next time the smoke appears."

Other than the wives in the cabins for married couples, the entire work center was now vacant. Everyone had an assignment or were on stand-by out on the district at different locations.

Randy came running out of the house and yelled to Ben, "hey I got a location for that fire, get your butt ready to go and meet me up by the gas pumps in five minutes." Ben grabbed his gloves and laced up his boots, grabbed his trusty beat up hardhat and headed up to the gas house.

Randy bellowed, "here put these C-rations in your pack, grab two canteens, a shovel and a Pulaski." Randy went inside and came out of the gas shed with an old-fashioned 6' two-man crosscut saw.

"Ben stared at the antique for minute shook his head and asked, "what the hell is that for, don't we have any power saws?"

Randy with his typical mean scowl on his face replied, "listen dipshit, the district only has five power saws available and they are in use by the fire guards. This is it for you and me." Randy then told Ben, "the fire is approximately 1/3-1/2 mile up the fence line above the work center, so let's get moving, we have at least five or six more hours of daylight, plenty of time."

Randy and Ben headed up the hill above the work center, walking along a fence line that was an allotment fence between two cattle grazing permits. There was a nice open path through the ponderosa pine forest.

The afternoon had suddenly started to show more buildup of clouds, typical for this time of the year with the promise of more late afternoon thunderstorms. The storm Ben survived during his earlier lookout adventure was an unusually severe early storm event for this area. Randy and Ben took off from the gas house with Ben carrying his canteen full of a gallon of water, C-rations, and two tools and so far, had no trouble hiking toward the fire. He was pretty proud of himself as he followed the six-foot five inch behemoth ahead of him carrying everything imaginable, the crosscut, oil, tools, water, and whatever else the big guy thought was necessary. The big jock of a basketball player strode effortlessly up the hill toward the smoke report. And the report was right on the money.

"Holy shit," exclaimed Ben as they hiked up over the last little rise. There in front of them, they both saw a 30" diameter ponderosa pine, about 100 feet tall. They could see the section that was burning three quarters of the way up. Small flames in the tree trunk were visible and smoke was curling up above the tree line.

"Crap, look at that damn thing up there, Randy bellowed in his usual voice, the problem is we have to fall this damn thing, buck it up, and then work on whatever is still burning after it hits the ground."

Randy looked over at Ben who weighed all of 140 pounds and pondered out loud, "have you ever used a crosscut? Look, here's the deal, we are going to fall this son of bitch right over there away from the fence line, and after it hits, we will put in a scratch line around anything burning, and then buck the damn thing up in two or three sections."

Randy looked over at the tree put his finger about 12" up and said, "here is where we will start the bottom of the undercut, we will cut a pie out of the face here and then do a back cut behind it and fall it over where I pointed earlier, OK? I'll get the saw started and you grab your handle and back and forth we will go for these two cuts of the undercut pie." Ben looked at the saw, as Randy started it through the tree, he could not believe how Randy got the saw to start literally gliding smoothly, as if on its own. Back and forth through the face of the tree the boys guided saw, spitting out large sawdust chunks the whole time.

And then Randy yelled, "get your ass in gear and grab on and let's get this thing going a little faster." The saw literally sang through the first horizonal part of the undercut and they finished it up rather quickly with Ben mostly just hanging on to the damn saw as Randy more or less kept the whole thing moving back and forth in the cut under his own power most of the time.

They both noticed the clouds starting to build up and the day get darker and darker as they took the saw out and positioned it to start the top part of the undercut which they would finish with a pie shaped piece of wood being kicked out. Thunder rumbled in the distance and Randy took out a file and started to knock down some rough edges on the saw's teeth. He bent over the saw blade and filed away, his hard hat barely hanging on and his cruiser's vest hanging down on his neck.

As Randy was hunkered over this filing operation, Ben heard some small 'thunk, thunk, thunk', noises as embers and tiny burning branches hit the back of the hunkered-over Randy's cruiser vest as he continued to merrily file away.

Finally, a larger ember hit Randy on the hardhat causing him to get totally pissed, as he yelled, "you stupid shit quit being a smart-ass while I am getting this damn thing sharp—no more kidding around when I am not looking."

Just then the largest ember still on fire and falling from the burned area high above, hit Randy right on top the hard hat as he was still looking at Ben. He yelled out, "shit that damn tree is starting to burn a little hotter up there with the wind blowing those friggin embers right down on us, we better get a move on and get it on the ground... Crap I thought you were screwing with me," he stated rather sheepishly.

The boys finished the undercut and Randy grabbed the Pulaski and with the axe end of the tool and chopped out the tiny bit of wood holding the pie-shaped cut. "All right he said, let's get the back cut going and get this damn thing on the ground." Randy placed the blade horizontally at the back of the tree with the undercut facing the targeted drop area and started the saw horizontally toward the front. Ben, once again, was barely holding on and not doing much of anything other than keeping the saw going back and forth, more of a guide than a sawyer as Randy once again pretty much muscled it through mostly under his power.

As the saw blade approached the undercut, they heard a cracking noise and the tree began to slowly tilt toward the landing zone, and then after a louder crack, Ben heard the loud shooshing noise as the 100-foot ponderosa pine crashed to the ground, slowly at first and then it finally crashed down for an accurately planned landing.

"Quick you grab that shovel and start a scratch line up where the burned-out area is," Randy yelled as the thunder was now too loud for normal conversation. Ben ran up the length of the tree and started a scratch line around the burning area, all the time looking for any burning embers on the ground scattered near the fallen tree. He quickly shoveled dirt on all the most dangerous embers and then continued digging down through the layer of pine needles. He quickly built a narrow fire line around the entire burning area, up around the treetop and back down where Randy was working a few yards out around the fallen tree. He figured he scratched out about 150' of line and smiled to himself with more than a little pride.

Randy chopped some of the smaller limbs off the tree and used the narrow "hoe" blade of the Pulaski to scrape away burned material keeping everything inside the fire line that Ben scratched right behind him.

"Hey," Randy yelled, "you did a damn good job getting that line in as quick as you did, not bad for a skinny little shit!" "After about three hours of scratching at the burned areas, bucking the downed tree into three sections and checking all around the fire line both inside and out looking for any burning materials, Randy stated emphatically, "I think this puppy is pretty much out."

"Let's grab a bite to eat now because there's not going to be any dinner down below and we'll need to keep an eye out for another hour for any smokes and then head back down to the Center, I'll call in from there that the fire is out,' Randy said. Randy and Ben walked back along the length of the fallen tree to the fence line, leaned their tools up against the barbed wire, hung the two canteens over a post and sat down to eat some C's.

A thunder cell has once again built up over them with gusty winds and they both quickly jumped up, and walked up and down the fallen tree, and took one more look around the fire line checking for smoke or flames before settling back down to eat. Flashes were now getting a little closer as they finished their c-rations and both were getting a little anxious about being so close to the top of the hill and leaning up against fenceposts during their meal.

"You know," Randy yelled out, "I think we better move away from this barbed wire over there near that little thicket of trees and away from these tall ones, there like lightning rods and we're the grounding." They quickly started to move away from the fence line. Ben felt his hair stand on end and his skin felt prickly and then suddenly out of nowhere a white bright intense flash of blinding light lit up the entire darkened forest and the thunder sounded like a hundred screaming locomotives, an explosion of sound and light, all happening at the same time.

CHAPTER 14

That bright flash once again caused Ben's mind to play tricks on him as he vividly remembered looking over at Specialist Inswell who was lying next to him behind sandbags near the corner of the building they were assigned to stand guard over. The sandbags were piled three or four high and around eight each direction at a right angle along the corner of the roof.

Ben whispered to Inswell, "You know this is damn serious because this is the first time, we have been given live ammo in seven months."

They both had the older M-14s rather than the newer M-16s which was fine with both of them as that is what they had in basic training. Bright flashes were occurring a few hundred meters out along the perimeter of the airbase and they could hear the ensuing explosions. Red tracer rounds could be seen going off all over the perimeter of the base as the explosions got louder and their flashes lit up the night sky.

Ben and Inswell kept a tight vigil watching the 10-foot tall, electrified fence below surrounding their compound and around the entryway in case any of the VC tried to scale it and break into the compound. More tracers were seen, and the cracking of machine gun and other automatic gunfire was only 100 meters away in the compound next door. A firefight was in progress on the other side of the building next door where they could not see who was doing what. They both started breathing loud enough they could hear each other's every breathe wondering if the VC would head toward their fenced in compound. They were both sure a lot of the explosions were from incoming rockets, rockets that were most likely launched from near their barracks compound. The noise and flashes from the rockets, RPGs, the burping sound from the mini-guns from Cobra gunships, and the even louder heavy sounds from nearby automatic weapons continued for a couple more hours before things finally settled down to just an occasional explosion.

Ben, whispered in a shaky voice, "I think we are going to be ok here, not so much gun fire and those heavier explosions have almost stopped."

Ben learned later that the airbase suffered heavy damage to planes, supplies, and several hangars, but most of the casualties were VC with scores killed along the perimeter fencing as very few actually breeched the perimeter. Those that did, only made it few steps before being gunned down. Across the entire country, the Tet offensive was a wake-up call to everyone, even though in the long run, American and ARVN forces were the victors as tens of thousands of VC were killed. Ben's tour of duty would never be the same. The war had now come to him and his unit, no more leisure Sundays from now on.

As quickly as the memories flooded in like an ocean tide, Ben's mind blended back to reality as he looked over at Randy, "you all right?" he yelled hoarsely, for some reason he now had a sore throat.

"I am ok but Jesus, that was damned close and the smell—can you smell it---ozone from the heat of the flash, I am guessing," Randy exclaimed with an unsteady voice. "I remember reading about lightning-created ozone in chemistry class."

They both stood up rather shakily and checked their clothing and boots, "I am OK," Ben offered, "nothing singed or burnt." "But man, he added, that whole thing practically made my skin crawl, I could feel it seconds before it hit," Ben stated in a more calm voice. The thunder cell had dissipated as quickly as it formed with the remnants moving off to the northeast.

Both went over to the fence line and Ben exclaimed, "Shit Randy, look at our tools!!" Both of the wooden handles of the Pulaski and the shovel were still leaning against the barbed wire and both had long black burn marks running down the handles toward the metal part of the two tools.

"Jesus," Randy replied, stammering a little, "that could have been us had we stayed close to the fence.

It looks like the lightning hit the barbed wire and travelled along the whole damn thing. And look at the canvas straps on the canteens—hell look at the damn canteens," he said as they looked what used to be bright orange canvas covers. The orange on them was now tinged with black marks and soot around both of them near the aluminum edges.

Ben looked over at Randy, who was now looking more pale than ever and offered, "well the good news is, we can show these singe/burn marks to anyone we talk to, because without this proof, I don't think anyone would believe what just happened, no matter how we told 'em---hell I can't hardly believe it myself and we just experienced it! Let's get hell out of here before another thunder cell forms."

Randy and Ben checked the fire one last time and headed back to the work center and the comforts of the old "ranger's house" both thinking how close they came to being toast like those two wooden tool handles. They could both see lightning strikes off in the distance and the storms were over the valley area all around the neighboring ranches and the work center. Randy knew that the evening may not see the end of new fires with all the new ground strikes on the District.

Ben plunked himself down on the living room's well-worn couch and took off his work boots and socks. "Shit, he yelled, "look at this." Randy rushed in to see what the hell was the matter and Ben pointed down to his feet, "look at those burns on the top of my feet and toes," he exclaimed. They were not bad burns, more like a light sunburn, but never-the-less, they definitely were from their close bout with the lightning bolt.

"Damn, Randy said looking down at the redness on both feet, "it's a good thing we moved when we did, hell we could have had some of the more important parts of our body singed," he smiled openly and started to laugh. He and Ben both laughed together in a somewhat lighter but nervous mood. But on their faces, both still kept looks of amazement after the day's events. As Ben settled down, he was starting to get a little worried about the recurring memories of his time overseas.

Those thoughts were interrupted as a few members of the engineering crew wandered in and Bill entered the room along with Rob. All of them had worked on several small lightning fires with most not much bigger than a 50' circle and a couple no bigger than the size of a garbage can lid, typical summer fire season.

After hearing Ben and Randy's incredible story, Bill offered up, "well in keeping with today's strange lightning events, you wouldn't believe what happened here either." Bill explained further, "we actually got back here fairly early, around 4:30 and even though the District was still getting lightning, it was mostly right around here, so we were ordered to standby here at the center, in case like you guys, we had another fire close by."

"Well," Bill continued, "so there we were sitting around waiting for the phone to ring which we could hear it do once in a while, most likely rings set off by lightning around the area. I told our dumb greenhorn to not answer the phone, especially since there was lightning in the area. We needed to be damn sure it was our rings, loud and clear, not an electrical charge from the storms, otherwise, we could end up toasted. Needless, to say, Rob, in his infinite wisdom, did not listen. The phone rang one long ring, rather loudly, it was not our ring, but hell no he had to run up and answer it."

Bill continued, "Like a dummy Rob ran in and picked up the phone just as a loud crack of lightning hit flashing throughout the whole house. Get this; it literally knocked his dumb ass across the kitchen over by the cookstove, near the garbage can."

"I yelled at him to see if he was all right—stupid question, he's never going to be all right." "I ran into the kitchen as he was getting his dazed dumb butt rather unsteadily off the floor.

And he kind of sheepishly stammered, "shit, Randy was right, don't go near the phone in a lightning storm." Rob continued loudly, "my damn ears are still ringing really loud and you all sound like you are talking from inside a tin can."

"I'll bet it was the same ground strike you guys barely dodged up on the hill. Hell, that fence comes right down here to the compound and up next to the house," Bill offered. Randy had been standing in the hallway listening to Bill's story and just started laughing in a loud jovial voice.

"You know, when I told you girls about that phone, the metal housing, the dry cell batteries, and the metal number 9 lines, did you think I was friggin kidding, especially you Rob? You need to listen a little closer and remember what the hell I tell you," he added still laughing. Randy went back into his bedroom, still giggling thinking to himself, my God will this summer ever end. I need a beer!"

CHAPTER 15

Finally, the fires were all out, no more lightning, and the weather was clear and warm. Everyone would be able to enjoy what little was left of the evening with no more standby ordered.

After the big lightning bust, another long week of work passed, "I think we should go to town this weekend, maybe to the drive-in," Ben offered as they all collapsed in the living room. I think we could all use a little diversion."

"We don't have a rig that all of us can ride in," Wes stated.

Bill wandered into the room and offered, "listen I am batching this weekend, wife and kids have gone over to her mom's house so the kids can see their grandparents. So, I am staying here this weekend, we can take my extended cab pickup, it'll hold six."

Randy grabbed Bill and said, "hey look, I know I have been a real hard-ass on the girls, but you know what, they have done really well these past couple of weeks. Take a couple quarts of my homebrew with you. They have earned it. But listen, I'll trust it to you but make sure they don't think I am getting soft and make sure they stay out of trouble."

Bill smiled and replied, "thanks, we'll enjoy some at the drive-in and I'll make sure no one gets carried away." Words Bill spoke with no clue how they would come back to haunt him.

Saturday evening rolled around and Wes, Bill, Rob, and Ben traded their work boots and clothes for 'tennies', shorts, and t-shirts as it would be a warm evening at the drive-in. Kahuna had left earlier safely in the hands of two different local girls, who picked him in up their parents' Eldorado convertible. Chris was heading back to Beeton for the weekend for his sister's birthday party.

"Hey," Bill said. "Look what I have, as he pulled out a cold quart bottle of beer from his little portable cooler? A small glass for the road, ok, perhaps another later on."

Rob looked at the other three and stated rather emphatically, "I don't do rot-gut crap as if he knew good from bad homebrew," "you guys try it and if you don't barf it up, I might have glass.

"Damn," Bill replied after a quick drink, "this is really good. Randy has come up with something like a cross between Country Club and Heidelberg—I like it!."

What Rob didn't want anyone to know what that he had only drank any type of drink with alcohol in it was once in his life and that was when he was given a tiny sip of the family's Mogen David on Christmas eve. Rob finally relented, "hey pour me a glass, looks like you guys haven't been poisoned." He grabbed the glass of foamy homebrew and gulped it down in two swigs. "Geez, that is not bad, not bad at all," he said with a light buzz already kicking in.

It was about an hour and a half before the ticket booth opened at the drive-in and with a 45-minute drive ahead of them Bill yelled at them, "let's load up and get down the mountain." Off they went, their small cooler in tow, Bill driving with Wes riding shotgun, Rob sitting behind Bill and Ben on the rear passenger side. They started talking about last weekend's activities and how they were all damn lucky to get their first real taste of real firefighting behind them.

Rob teasing Ben and feeling the effects of his jugged-down glass of beer looked at Ben, "Hey, so how did you really get your toes sunburned. You and Randy take a nap with your boots and socks off?"

"Not funny, not funny' at all, Ben responded. At least I didn't get my ass knocked off trying to be an indoor lightning rod. '

"Hell, what do you expect from a moron," Bill piped in.

That was all it took for Rob, the last straw as he light-headedly reached up and grabbed Bill around the neck and started choking him. "You asshole, get your gawd damn hands off me before we crash down that canyon, you stupid clod!!"

"Take it back you hick cowboy loser, or I'll make you damn sorry," stated Rob. He loosened his grip just a little and Bill gasped a little. Ben turned toward Rob and hit him with a kidney-punch as hard as he could. Everyone could hear a loud painful guttural cry coming from Rob as he loosened his grip on Bill completely and slumped forward in his seat.

"Shit Ben," Rob exclaimed, "what the Hell, why did you do that, I was only kidding."

Wes turned around, shook his fist at Rob and shouted, " listen you dumbass, we do not kid around on this road, you know how many people have died down in that canyon, keep your damn kidding to your self---choking is not kidding. You ever do that again, and you will be answering to me and you'll get more than one punch to the guts, do you understand me— never do that he again!' he repeated to Rob slowly.

Rob slowly collapsed backward into his seat, still feeling the pain on his right side and answered, "you guys need to quit calling me moron and start treating me better he answered, stammering like a little kid. I think the beer must have made me do it, I am a little dizzy."

"More than a little dizzy," Bill stated and he actually started to laugh now that things were calming down.

Rob, tapped Bill on the shoulder, "sorry, OK, sorry."

CHAPTER 16

With the drama of the drive down the mountain finally over, the boys arrived at the drive-in movie ticket booth. They hid the small cooler with the other two quarts of beer and some jerky out of sight. Not only was there a no alcohol policy at the drive-in, but there was also a policy against bringing in any outside food or drink of any kind. Bill collected money from the boys for their share and paid the young lady inside the ticket shack for the carload, as it was actually cheaper that way. They were told to go toward the back, since the pickup had a high cab, but the good news is, she told them turn your truck around and back into your spot, it's easier to see from the bed than those front and back seats. *A good idea*, Bill thought, as he had several wool blankets under the back seat they could use for cushioning.

They found a place in the middle near the last few rows and slowly backed the truck up near a speaker stand and stretched the speaker into the bed where they could all hear the music playing before the movie starts. "Hey Ben," Bill asked, why don't you go up with me to the concession stand and we'll get four small cokes."

"I don't like Coke, Rob stated."

"That's OK, Bill added, we'll use the cups for our beer. No one will know or suspect we have beer in a red coke or green seven-up cup." Ben agreed and he and Bill walked the 30 yards up to the concession stand. On the way there, it seemed like everyone he had ever met or knew was here at the drive-in. They saw the big boss, old hook-nose John, and his wife Jeane. Ranger Bash was ahead of him at the concession stand. Bill nodded his head to Ben, isn't that Red the married engineer next door in the little green cabin and his foxy wife Rina?"

The concession stand was freshly painted and located just below the film projectors which were housed in the upstairs booth. The restrooms were around behind in the back of the small building. They each took two cups of pop and a couple tubs of popcorn back to their rig and settled in waiting for the movie to start.

And it was going to be a great movie, "Bullitt," starring Steve McQueen. Ben could hardly believe this small-town drive-in was already showing such a top-rated and popular movie and of course Steve McQueen was one of his favorite actors.

The first half of the movie was absolutely the greatest and the boys stretched and sat up a little straighter as the lights around the drive-in slowly lit up for the 15-minute intermission.

Ben pointed over to his left toward a solid black Eldorado, "hey isn't that Kahuna for there?"

Bill and Wes both turned to look and Wes said, "good gawd yes, and look at the two good looking girls with him, and in the back seat no less. I just cannot believe it." He has some kind of knack for conning those locals into whatever the heck he wants, amazing!"

"Let's enjoy that other beer now, Bill volunteered, we've earned an extra glass this week. Look, hold your coke glasses low below the pickup fender and I'll sneak a pour for all of you, then we can take the bottle and hide it in these popcorn tubs and one of us can dump it up in that garbage can by the concession stand after the movie starts up again." Bill measured out the same amount to each of the four as best he could while keeping it all on the sly. Once he finished they could drink it out in the open while sitting there in the pickup bed.

"You OK moron---er Rob, sorry!!," he asked.

"You know," Rob responded, I could actually get to like this stuff."

Ben thought to himself *what a helluva picture that would be having this dude drinking beer all the time, no thanks.* The movie was about to start up again and after a few minutes so Ben quickly offered to take the evidence up to the garbage can and get rid of it before someone got wise and turned them in. Ben took off slowly walking up to the garbage cans with the empty quart beer bottles hidden in two paper tubs from the popcorn.

As he approached, the dimly lit concession area and the garbage cans, he noticed the local version of Barney Fife. *Shit*, he thought, *there was Sgt. Dusty, as he was called by all the locals.* He was standing next to the closest concession window trying to order a soft drink. Ben slowly sauntered up and dropped his hopefully hidden beer bottles in the can. Thump, and then clang, the glass bottles rang out as they hit the side of the can. And of course, good old Sgt. Dusty, always looking for a non-existent crime, peered over the top of the can and spotted the empty homebrew bottles.

Ben turned and slowly walked around the corner toward the men's restroom at the back of the concession stand, all the time glancing back to see if the good Sgt. was following. And wouldn't you know it, he was. Ben's mind was now racing a little as he wondered to himself if it was actually illegal to drink beer at the drive-in, or was it just a local rule, or whatever, he wondered to himself? He did not want to get on the wrong side of the locals no matter what. He wanted to be here on this Forest for quite some time as he was starting his career. It would not be good he thought if he was confronted with the smell of beer on his breathe along with the empty homebrew containers by the good Sgt.

Even with a few clouds overhead obscuring the moon, it was still light enough for Ben to see a narrow cow path leading up the slight rise behind the concession stand. He quickly turned away from the restroom, onto the path and followed it about ten yards over a slight rise and then down toward what looked like another little pathway. The moon was now completely obscured by a cloud as Ben hightailed it over to the next pathway. This trail was not a trail at all but rather a four-foot wide and five-foot deep irrigation ditch that ran for several miles parallel the highway behind the drive-in. Ben was glad he spotted it before the light faded as he hopped over the ditch, barely getting to the other side. He glanced back behind him and just coming over the rise was Barney Fife's twin, Sgt. Dusty. The good Sgt. approached the ditch, Ben veered off to the left along the ditch and quickly put some distance between the two.

Sgt. Dusty, being the clueless dude that he is, sped forward down the path and all Ben heard was a loud splash, followed by a very loud "SON-OF-A-BITCH!" as Sgt Dusty ended up in the ditch. He was greeted by chest-deep cold water, clear up to his badge. His boots were stuck in the clay mud on the ditch bottom, his gun and ammo were soaked, and his flashlight was nowhere to be found. Ben stopped and hid behind a small juniper watching Sgt. Dusty try to grab grass or brush clumps and pull his way up the steep banks of the ditch. But all he did was slip back each time and getting muddier, all to no avail.

Finally, after several more outbursts of four-letter words, he gave up and sloshed through the water walking along the ditch for a few feet until he found a small juniper tree near the edge. He slowly pulled himself on his belly up on the bank on the wrong side of the ditch. "SHIT," he yelled out loud to no one, "now I got to jump back across the damn thing," he muttered to himself."

Ben quickly slipped away as the good Sgt. looked for an easier route back to the concession stand area. Ben jogged quietly along the ditch toward the drive-in front gate and slipped in past the closed ticket shack and back to the truck. The whole thing could not have taken more than six or seven minutes, but to Ben, it felt like an hour.

"Where the hell you been?" Bill whispered loudly.

"You would not believe what just happened," Ben offered and burst out laughing. He explained to the boys the whole story, the clanging beer bottles, the slow pathway chase to the ditch, "Barney Fife" in the water up to his ass and eyeballs, as Ben exaggerated. They all expressed their disbelief in the whole story but the laughing took a while to die down.

Rob who finished laughing first, piped up, "Hey I am still a little woozy from that beer and I need to go whiz, I'll be right back."

CHAPTER 17

The movie finished and the drive-in which had been completely filled with half the town's cars and trucks, started to unwind. Slowly everyone began to make their way down the rows sideways from the screen angling toward the exit.

"Damn," Wes exclaimed, "where the hell is our idiot partner in crime?"

It was then the boys realized that Rob had been gone a full 15 minutes to 'go whiz' still feeling the effects of the homebrew.

"Shit," Bill reminded us, "that tenderfoot-greenhorn never has had much alcohol in his whole life and I'm beginning to think it may have him a little out of kilter."

"Really," Wes responded, "how the hell further out-of-kilter can that numbskull be, he sure as Hell isn't even close to normal without the beer."

Bill, Wes, and Ben waited a few more minutes as the drive-in was now half empty as cars made their way out the front gate. Bill, finally getting a little exasperated, said, "I'll go to the restroom and see if the idiot fell in. Otherwise, I have no clue where he could be."

Ben answered, "We'll take a look around here, I see Kahuna and his chicks haven't left maybe he wandered over there."

Ben sauntered over to Kahuna, still sitting in the backseat between the two very nice-looking young local girls. "Hey Kahuna," he asked, "did our idiot crewmember come over to see you guys. He left the truck about 10-15 minutes ago and we haven't seen him since. He said the alcohol made him woozy, shit, he had one glass of beer over an hour ago!"

Kahuna responded, "Haven't seen him, thank God. I have enjoyed the time with these two lovely young things and sure as heck didn't any of his drama."

"OK," Ben said, "we'll wait as long as we can but we have to leave after the last car, because they shut this place down and lock her up.

Ben returned to the truck and joined the other two as Bill had already returned.

Bill reminded everyone, "We need to leave right after that last car over there, because they will lock the place up right afterwards. We can take a look around the entrance area to the drive-in and see if he wandered up or down the road toward the mill."

Following the last car out, the boys drove slowly down the gravel road that led from the drive-in to the highway, looking at every bush and around each tree, they searched closely to see if Rob was hiding, passed out, or just plain wandering around. They did not see him anywhere along the drive-in access road and after turning down along the highway, they drove slowly away from town hoping to find Rob in all his stupid glory. Not seeing him, they turned the car around and headed back toward the direction of the sawmill near town, passing the drive-in entrance once again.

About a third of mile from the drive-in was the County's largest sawmill with its huge millpond shining in obscuring moonlight off on the side. The millpond was left over from an old rock and gravel site and was over a 100 feet deep in places. It was full of logs ready to be drawn up into the mill by the log conveyor. The large parking area at the mill was empty as the last shift ended and the next shift was not until 5:00am.

Bill looked over at the millpond, "Look how that little bit of fog is hanging over the water. See that light pole and that little outhouse-looking shack. There's always a night watchman over on duty, let's go see if he has seen our idiot missing in action."

The boys drove up close to the guard shack and Steve Johnson, the 75-year-old watchman, slowly limped out to see what these punks, as he called all young people, wanted.

"What the Hell you punks doing here, you ain't supposed to be on mill property. Nobody is allowed around here; what the hell you want?"

Bill explained their missing member's story and the fact he may have wandered this far from the drive-in and that the beer might have made him a little weird, more so than he already was.

Lightning was now starting to flash off in the distance and clouds were starting to form overhead.

The watchman responded, "Haven't seen anyone, just me and my trusty transistor listening to a little music, now get your punk butts out of here before I call Sgt Dusty."

As the boys turned and headed back to the truck, they heard a faint voice muttering and humming.

Watchman Johnson blurted, "What the heck is that sounds like it's coming from the pond. It's hard to see with that steam fog on the warm pond water."

The four wandered over to the edge of the mill pond and they could not believe their eyes. Out toward the center of the pond sat their resident idiot of the house, Rob. He was straddling a large diameter log out in the middle of the pond oblivious to the world, just kind of muttering and half-way humming to himself or anyone else within earshot.

Ben look around through the fog and noticed that there was a walkway not too far from Rob's watery perch. It consisted of two logs cabled together with a couple of boards nailed along them to walk on. The walkway stretched out covering four or five pairs of the logs with boards. Along this walkway, Ben could see other logs floating nearby and he figured the walkway was used to sort the floating logs for cutting, probably based on grade and species.

Ben yelled back at Wes, "Hey, we can walk up here to within 20 feet of the idiot and pull his log over with that 'pike' pole. I think it's one of those 24 footers, should be long enough to reach."

Even though Rob was less than 20 feet from the walkway, it was still a little hard to see him clearly through the hazy steam-like fog, along with heavier nighttime thunder clouds starting to cover the moon.

"Come here and help me," Ben yelled at Wes.

Ben turned to where Rob was and called out, "Hey, dipshit, I am going to reach out with this pike pole and pull your log over here so you can get out on the walkway, OK?"

Rob answered in a barely-understandable low voice, "Leave me the Hell alone. You guys hate me; you don't want me around, just go and let me be.." He answered in a slurred, whiney, self-indignant voice.

Watchman Johnson blurted out, "Get that little shit off my millpond right now or I will call the cops. I have no time for this shit and that little punk needs to get his ass off my pond—now!"

"All right, all right, give me a minute, Ben responded. "Wes, come over here while I reach out with this pole."

Ben grabbed the aluminum pike pole in hopes of snaring the end of the log Rob was straddling. The pole had a small hook on the end for snagging and sorting logs. Ben tried to catch the hook on the end of the log to no avail. A pike pole that long has quite a bit of sag to it which made reaching out that far extremely difficult.

The lightning in the distance was now much closer making Ben's need to snag the log all the more urgent, and the floodlight over the pond was starting to flicker off and on. Ben reach out one more time and caught something and pulled it hard.

Just as he latched onto something, the lights went completely dark. Ben and Wes heard the sound of something near the log as Ben finally could feel the pole snagging into the log. The sound was kind of a muffled sloshing sound. They both squinted through the haze and darkness as the lights kept flickering off and on, and then were momentarily completely out.

Ben exclaimed, "Holy Shit, where is he? The light came back on. And Ben blurted out, "He's not on the log and I can't see him in the water!"

"What the Hell," Wes cried out, "What did you do Ben?"

"What do you mean what did I do? I just snagged the front of the log. The hook was in the bark a little and then something made it turn loose. It almost felt like that dumb ass might have pulled the hook out of the bark. Even with the lights back on, I can't see anything, can you?" Ben exclaimed.

Night watchman Johnson yelled out to Ben and Wes, "What's going on? What happened out there?" Even though out there was only 50 feet from the guard shack. "Did you grab that that little shit's log and pull him in?"

Ben felt a little sick to his stomach and yelled back, "You better call the cops; that idiot's not on the log and I can't see him anywhere."

Bill returned from searching around the millpond edge for any sign of Rob. He listened to Ben and Wes as they told him about reaching out with the pike pole in the dark catching an end of the log and then the small hook either coming loose on its own or perhaps pulled out by the beer-woozy Rob.

"Old man Johnson just called the cops to come down and help us search for him," Ben said. "I absolutely cannot figure out what the hell just happened; I had the damn log!"

Bill looked directly at Wes and Ben and asked, "Now listen you two, as much as we don't like Rob's worthless butt, you didn't give him a little push with that pole, did you?"

Ben looked at Wes and then at Bill, "Jeez, hell no, he might be a dumb peckerhead, but I would never do anything like that. You gotta remember, I want to complete my probation period on this job and continue here with a fulltime career. I would never do anything to jeopardize any of that. Man, I could be so screwed now," Ben stammered.

A few minutes later, Sgt Dusty drove up to the guard shack and came over to the boys, "Hey what the hell are you all doing at the mill site this time of night?"

Johnson looked over at the Sergeant, "Well, seems like these little punks lost one of their buddies out there on the mill pond. He was out on a log babbling and humming. I was told and these boys reached out with that pike pole over there and tried to hook the log he was riding and pull him over there"

He pointed to the log walk. "Somehow," Johnson added, they lost him. "He either slipped off the log, slid off the log, or was shoved off the log. I have no clue. I heard it all, but it was really hard to see over there from where I was with all the foggy haze hanging over the water and the power going off and on. There were no lights at times."

"Which one of you was the pole operator," the Sgt. asked with a smirk on his face? Looking directly at Ben, he added, "Do I know you; you look familiar? Have I had you in jail before?"

"No," Ben stated emphatically.

Ben couldn't help but notice the clean fresh and pressed uniform, no pistol, no ammo pack, and no flashlight, just cuffs and a night stick were hanging from his belt. And the good Sgt was wearing some kind of brown loafers that obviously were not part of his uniform. Ben quickly hid a smile that came over him, and explained to the Sgt in great detail exactly what happened. How he found the pike pole lying on the log walkway, grabbed it, tried twice to hook Robs log and pull him in, how the lights were off and on. He explained how he caught part of the bark with the small hook on the second or third try and somehow as he started to pull the log Rob toward safety; he explained that it came loose, either on its own or with a little help from Rob.

Sgt Dusty rushed away from the scene over to his squad car and radioed his headquarters, which was the local police station on the other end of town. He asked for assistance in the form of a search party, the bloodhound they had trained as a tracker, and a diver for the morning. Riverton police had two volunteers that were certified as qualified divers that could search the pond after sunrise. Briefly the Sgt explained over the radio what had happened. Of course, the boys never mentioned the homebrew, or the fact that Rob might be a little nuts, or at the very least a little unstable.

CHAPTER 18

I t was now about one o'clock in the morning.
Ben, Wes, and Bill sat slumped in the pickup
with the doors wide open wondering what could
possibly have happened to Rob. There was no
thrashing sound coming from the water, absolutely
no sound that might be attributed to someone in
distress or worse case, drowning. With the three in
deep thought and starting to get more than a little
scared, the tracker bloodhound and its handler
showed up at the scene.

The handler was a tall thin kid, probably an
auxiliary-type volunteer Ben thought, 19 at the oldest.
He came over and introduced himself, "Hey guys, I'm
Jack Smith, and this is Beau my hound. I am going to
take him around the end of the millpond and see if
we can pick up a scent."

"Do you have anything in the truck that belonged
to this dude that I could have Beau sniff, anything at
all that belongs to this guy," he asked.

Bill responded, "I don't think so." He looked
around. Wait, I think he left his baseball cap in the

backseat, let me look around. Bill went back to the truck and looked around and finally found Rob's hat where it had been accidently kicked toward the corner of the pickup bed. "Here, this is his hat, he left it in the back of the rig when he went to the bathroom at the drive-in, at least that's where he said he was going."

Jack responded, "Hey, that will work just great," as he held the hat under the nose of Beau.

Jack and his hound took off and started circling around the truck and then out along the edge of the millpond. The millpond was around five acres in size and it would take the hound less than 60 minutes to cover the entire perimeter.

The two disappeared around the far side of the millpond with good old Beau nose to the ground sniffing, snorting, and eagerly searching along the water's edge. After about 10 minutes, everyone listened up as they heard Beau's howling barks from the other side of the pond. He had picked up the scent of something and had drug Jack away from the pond about 25 yards in the opposite direction, toward the foothills that surrounded the mill. Just as quickly as Jack's trusty hound, Beau, picked up on something, he stopped and lost interest. Beau circled around the area where he stopped, sniffing every square inch and---nothing.

****

Forty-five minutes later after Beau has sniffed everything and anything, the hound and Jack returned to the shack area. Jack spoke first, "Look Beau never misses and about two-thirds of the way around, he caught the scent of something. At least it was a scent he thought was related to the smells from his hat. We headed over there toward that hill and just as quickly as Beau found it, he lost the scent or it just plain ended and he could not find a trace anywhere to start up again."

Ben asked, "Does that mean Rob crawled out of the pond and took off somewhere?"

"Not necessarily," Jack responded, "Beau and I have only been doing this on 'practice training' cases, so this is the first time we have tried to find a real person. It could mean anything. I think we're going to have to call in a more experienced tracking dog from the Sheriff's Department. They have a pair of dogs that have been successful in searches for missing hikers, kids, and other cases around the county. It's getting late, I'll have the station call the Sheriff's office when I get back down there, then I'm heading home. Us volunteers still have to work real jobs!"

Sgt Dusty told Ben, Wes, and Bill to head over to the Police Station and someone would take their statements about what they saw and what actually happened. He wanted to hear everything that went down that day and anything they could relate that may answer why Rob would either run away, kill himself, or…?

****

The three started to feel the weight of what had happened and the fact that it was the middle of the night, as they apprehensively strolled into the station.

There was a young duty officer pouring a cup of coffee near a small sink and he told the boys, "You three come over here sit around this table. Do not talk to each other or look over each other's statements. I want each of you to separately write down the events of the day and the evening; put down anything that might have happened that's important earlier in the day or later, and make it as detailed as possible."

After about an hour, they had completed their statements and as directed, signed and dated them, and added the exact time of completion.

"Can we go back to the work enter now," Bill asked?

Sgt Dusty walked in, " Yeah, you can take off, I got your boss, Ranger Bash, out of bed and explained the situation as best we know. I told him I needed you two back here in the morning. He agreed to that and told me to let you know, you will be on paid leave tomorrow. You will come back here tomorrow morning at 8:30 am. We'll have the Sheriff's hounds try and figure things out. If we find nothing, I am going to have to call this punk's parents. Do you know who they are," he asked?

Ben told him what little he knew; that he thought the guy's dad was some kind of Congressman or

Judge or some high-falooting political type. He lived somewhere within a 100 or so miles of Baltimore, and that he was not being really sure.

Bill offered, "You can call the personnel people at the District Office. They have all that in his personnel stuff when he signed up. We all had to put home address, next of kin, or nearest relative type information on the forms.

CHAPTER 19

All three were quiet as church mice as Bill drove up the winding mountain road back to the workstation.

Bill broke the silence, "Listen Ben, I will ask you this for the last time, did you shove that little S.O.B. into the pond on purpose? All of us at one time or another in the past few weeks wished he would just go away or disappear."

Ben was still a little dazed thinking of the night's events; having beer at the drive-in, narrowly escaping the clutches of Sgt Dusty, who he was sure had figured out it was him that got him ditch swimming. *And then there was Rob, that dumb little shit. He is screwing us over once again; but how, why, and where the Hell is he?* Ben wondered.

"Not only no, but Hell no," Ben replied. "Listen as much as I did not care for that sissy little worm, I would not harm him and other than that last little bit of crap heading to the drive-in, he was finally acting at least half-way decent. So, the answer is, don't ask me again, I have no clue what happened out there."

Bill, who had a wife and four kids, was starting to get a little worried about his own future. He wanted to believe Ben, but that choking episode, the lantern episode, and who knows how many others, made him wonder if Ben didn't just take advantage of the situation and shove him right off that log with the pike pole. And then just as quickly, Bill decided, *No Ben loves the local area, wants a career and I believe him. Perhaps tomorrow will bring more answers as to what happened out on that pond.*

****

Morning took forever but sleeping in until 7:00 felt good to Ben. They were usually up an hour or two earlier but, no work today was OK by him. Well he thought so, until he remembered why.

The three quickly ate breakfast and headed back down the mountain to the police station. There, they met Sgt. Dusty, who had them follow his squad car, as they all went back to the mill pond site.

The mill was running, under the watchful eye of another police officer, actually the only other fulltime cop in the small town. He was watching where the logs entered the mill to make sure nothing was attached to the any, such as the missing person's clothing.

There was a millpond worker with the same 24-foot aluminum pike pole sorting logs and keeping an eye out for anything suspicious. The plan was to shut the operation completely down for their 10:00 a.m.

morning shift break and have the two divers in the water searching for Rob's body.

Sgt. Dusty told the boys, "The Sheriff's two volunteer divers and their hound team will be here within the hour. Is there anything else you guys can think of or remember that might give us a clue as to what went down---or why?"

They shook their heads and responded that they couldn't think of a thing.

Dusty added, "By the way, I did get ahold of this punk's father. Shit he is a State Senator in New York and quite wealthy and influential. He is extremely upset. He took a Redeye flight last night. He is driving straight from the airport and he should be here later this morning."

****

The two seasoned bloodhounds and their expert handler found nothing different around the mill site. The scent went out away from the pond and then back toward the water and then just disappeared. As far as the divers, they too had no luck in finding anything in the pond. There was no sign of any clothes or remains, or anything. Although the water was definitely murky, they could see most, but not all, of the area with their underwater lights. They searched around the sunken logs and other obstacles that the lights could reach. It was a definite puzzle how Rob could vanish into thin air, especially since he was half drunk and half crazy.

Sgt. Dusty looking at the three suspects and emphatically stated, "All right look you three, I want you to go down to the station and wait. The missing person's father will be there in about an hour. Don't talk to each other about this investigation or anything you individually wrote in your statements. I want the facts fresh from your own little pea-brains when the father talks with you and me, understood?"

Ben looked over at Wes and Bill and kind of stammered, "Ok, we'll do as you asked, but look, we have no clue just like you what could have happened to Rob."

****

The boys hopped into Bill's pickup truck and headed across the small town, past their favorite 'Fire Drill' highway intersection and back to the Riverton Police Station. There they sat, mostly in silence, with feelings of unexplained queasiness awaiting the rich Eastern politician.

Ben was feeling especially anxious as he wondered, *Could I have shoved that SOB into the water with that pole, after all, I had a couple beers too, and he is a screaming asshole?*

His self-doubt was soon interrupted by a loud voice from the police station doorway, "Who the Hell is in charge here?" demanded the tall stranger. He was a very handsome older gentleman, well dressed in a dark suit and red tie, expensive custom-made leather shoes, and impeccably manicured nails.

CHAPTER 20

Wow, Ben thought, this guy has to be Rob's dad; soft white skin, no callouses anywhere on his body, styled hair, never been out of an office a day of his life. Sgt. Dusty walked over and introduced himself. They went into his office and the Sgt. explained what little facts he had.

They could see Rob's dad's face turn red, as he started gesturing, pointing and loudly exclaiming his dismay at the lack of information about the disappearance of his son. He demanded to know what has been done and why they haven't found Rob in this little podunk community.

The boys heard him yell, loudly, "Where the hell can anyone hide in this god-damned dump, for chrissakes. If you can't find him, bring in the State Police or FBI; anyone with experience besides you small town idiots! And I want to talk to those three dumb asses who were with him."

Sgt. Dusty yelled out, "You three get your butts in here and talk to this man. He needs to know what happened and you three were there, it's on you."

Ben, Wes, and Bill entered the office where Rob's father and the Sgt. had been discussing and cussing.

Rob's father was visibly upset, but Ben marveled how he reminded him of his grandfather. He was all decked out in an everyday suit, vest, coat and tie, and had on almost identical, custom-made shoes. *Amazing*, he thought.

Rob's dad blurted out, "Ok you three, what the hell happened and where the hell is my son, Aaron?"

All three looked at each and in almost a united chorus replied, "Who the hell is Aaron?"

The father now was losing his patience and getting more red-faced by the minute. Little beads of sweat were streaking out of his white, perfectly combed hair, and down his forehead, as he blurted out, "What do you mean who's Aaron. He is my damned son, the one you have been living with, the one you did something to!"

"You mean Rob," Ben answered with a look of puzzled amazement. "We don't know any Aaron. We do know Rob was from somewhere around Baltimore. He was a typical greenhorn and a little on the crazy side; well maybe more than a little."

Aaron's dad slumped into a chair in front of Sgt. Dusty's desk and Murmured, "Shit I thought he was going to get better out here." "Look boys his name is Aaron Katz; we live in upstate New York. He was

142

having some emotional issues after his mother died two years ago. He has been under psychiatric care most of that time. If he takes his meds he is just fine, if not, well perhaps you may have seen his changes in behavior and rapid mood-swings.

Ben and the others took turns explaining to the distraught father everything that happened over the summer. They detailed the events of that final day and evening with, 'Rob'. They left nothing out, especially all the stupid things Rob had done. Finally, they talked about Saturday and going to the drive-in, the couple of glasses of beer they all had, and the subsequent disappearance of Rob----Aaron, that evening.

"Look," Ben cautiously explained, "I do not have a clue what happened. Like I said earlier, I put the pike pole on the log to pull him in. The lights went out and we heard a slight muffled sloshing sound along with the distant thunder. It did not sound like someone out there drowning. There was no cry for help; just a very slight sound of water splashing a little. I would not do anything to hurt anyone," Ben restated, "I want to work here permanently and I sure as hell wouldn't jeopardize that."

Aaron's father, who now had tears in his eyes, responded quickly, "I think I believe the three of you. Aaron has had so many emotional issues these past two years and he has done some things that---well-- were not something a 'normal' person would do. If he had a couple of beers, as you say, which by the way he has never had in his life, and took his Valium close to the same time, who knows what the effects would be. He was warned by his Doctor in New York to never mix anything with his Valium. He was taking a rather large dose and any alcohol would not sit well."

Bill looked at Aaron's father and remembered, "Look if it makes you feel any better, after that little choking incident coming down the mountain for the movie, Rob, er, Aaron did actually apologize, so there was some semblance of normalcy as we headed into town."

****

The three boys finally got back to Mineral Creek, well after dark. They were physically and mentally exhausted from what had transpired. It was not only the disappearance of Rob that was so tiring, but also finding out who he was and the big lie he lived under while there. Also, the meeting with Aaron's emotionally distraught and upset father had left them drained. Near the end of their conversation, Aaron's father seemed half-way gracious after thanking the boys for their honesty. But Ben could tell, he still didn't think they were all the way straight with him.

Ben's thoughts were interrupted by Kahuna's chariot. The big, black Eldorado had just driven up to the gate and those same two beautiful young ladies each gave Kahuna a kiss on the cheek before he bounded out of the car, smiling from ear to ear.

"Another wonderful time was had by all," Kahuna blurted out. Amused by his own words, he was not worried that he missed work on Monday.

"How the hell do you do it,?" Wes asked.

"Not sure," Kahuna answered, "could be my good looks, my great hair, or my muscles and suntan."

Gawddd, Ben thought, *what an ego, but whatever it is, it works for him.*

Kahuna yelled over to Ben, "Didn't you have any of those olive-skinned black-haired beauties in 'Nam share a little of their selves with you?"

"Really? Ben replied, "That is kind of personal and probably none of your damn business. I think I will head to bed; it has been a helluva weekend and I am glad we are going to work tomorrow. You guys can explain what Kahuna missed while he was playing tongue-swap with his two new friends.

Bill and Wes filled Kahuna in on the details of the weekend as Ben drifted off to sleep.

CHAPTER 21

But sleep didn't come easily, as he once again thought about Vietnam, the things that happened, the work he did, and finally the women he befriended, one in particular.

Her name was Mia, which she told him was pronounced Meeuh, and she was beautiful, about five-foot-one inches and no more than a 110 pounds. She had that beautiful, long, black hair you see in pictures of Asian women, and her skin was lighter than most of the women there. Her mother was half-Vietnamese / half-French and her father might have been Chinese. That made for an interesting combination, as her eyes were almost as round as Ben's and they were a light hazel color.

She wore the traditional *ao dai* dress all the time, which consisted of long, silk pants under an equally long, silk, tight-fitting dress. He thought about how beautiful those colors were on all the women, with blues, pinks, and other pastels mixed in with white.

That dress, Ben thought, *it just hung on her every curve like a it was molded to her body.*

He remembered where he first met Mia; it was in the restaurant-bar close to where they were almost bicycled-bombed. Even though her parents were fairly well off, she lived by herself, earned her own money working weekends, and went to the University of Saigon part-time. She was not some 'tea girl' looking for some GI or fat cat contractor to pay for play. Many of his friends that were bar girls came in from the countryside to make money any way they could, in the bar, in the bed, or as some Officer's hootchmate.

Ben finally dozed off to sleep. His dream quickly became as vivid as the reality of today's events. He dreamed that he was back in Cholon, some months back-- with Mia.

He had returned on a Sunday day-off to the restaurant-bar where Mia was working. The old Mama San who was in charge of the girls gave Ben her usual dirty look. He smiled and nodded and took out some piaster bills and handed Mia around 200 piasters for her Tea, roughly 75 cents US, give or take. That should keep the old girl shut up for at least an hour.

Mia said, "I am so glad you come today. I not do good on some of my English. Hard time in class."

Ben responded, "Why don't I try and help with some of your English. I can come by where you live and help; maybe next Sunday if I am off duty, unless of course you are working." Mia responded with a warm smile and answered, "Maybe more than study? You like me?"

Ben, in his usual shyness responded, "Of course I do, I just...."

"Shhh," Mia whispered, "I good girl, but you nice to me, unlike GIs who just want boom-boom and then disappear, gone forever after bed."

****

Ben continued to toss and turn all night long as his thoughts of Mia returned over and over. His continual dreams and sometimes nightmares took the place of a deep sleep. But, throughout the night, he remembered that next wonderful Sunday, as if it were yesterday.

Mia had told him which alley to go down, "Then you have to turn left," she said, "and when you reach canal, turn right and count number of doors. I am number four door down that little alley, away from the canal. Can you remember?"

On that day, Ben finished his shift, got his bunk area inspection completed and headed to Cholon, right at dusk. He found the alley and walked down it around a hundred meters. It seemed like forever. Then, when he got to the canal and turned right, he counted four doors, and knocked lightly on the fourth one.

Mia answered the door, she was wearing a pair of shorts and a pink t-shirt-like top, was barefooted, and absolutely gorgeous as the full moon lit up her smiling face.

"Come in quickly, before anyone see you," she whispered. "Not everyone here like Americans. Sometimes if they see Vietnam girl with GI, they report to VC."

Her little shack consisted of a couple of small rooms. There was a tiny entry room with a large crockery jar of water sitting on the floor and a bedroom with barely enough room for a bed. Behind her was a little kitchen area next to a bathroom of some kind. The bed was a short, homemade platform, with a mattress on top. The little bathroom was the size of a closet next to the bedroom, it consisted of a stool and some buckets.

She grabbed Ben by the hand and gently led him into the bedroom. He looked at her and for the first time had actually started to become physically aroused. His face started to feel a little flushed and he felt a little embarrassed that he might be turning a little red.

Mia smiled at him, "Hey nice GI Ben, you not have woman before?" Her voice was a little mischievous and caught Ben off guard.

"Yes I have," he said. Then his voice trailed off-- - "once."

Mia once again grabbed his hand and pulled him into the bedroom and onto the bed. She gave him a quick peck on his flushed cheek and said, "Take off your clothes, I be right back."

Ben forgot about any studying getting done and nervously took off his clothes, laid them neatly near the doorway, and plopped his buck-naked body under the sheet. He and that old sheet were the only thing on the bed besides an old, worn pillow. Mia came in, she had nothing on but that pretty pink t-shirt and Ben could see her small breasts moving up and down under its cover. She pulled the sheet off Ben, looking down at his full arousal, and chuckled, "GI what you do, you grow."

Without warning she hopped on top of Ben, but he stopped her and sheepishly stammered, "Let me get my rubber out of my pants pocket."

Mia looked at him and became visibly very angry stated, "No rubber, I good girl, no need, I do not sleep with dirty men...No! I go to school, learn to keep myself safe and clean and no babies—you hear?"

Ben nodded, rolled onto his back and Mia slid over the top of him and quickly had him inside her before he knew what was happening. Ben looked up at her as she started moving up and down and he ran his hands under her shirt and over her tiny, but shapely breasts, both topped with large nipples which seemed to be eagerly reaching out to his fingers on their own.

"No," she said, "Not that, no can touch again."

They took turns being the one on top or the bottom for the next two hours, stopping only to drink water and wipe the sweat from each other; at least wherever he was allowed to touch her.

Panting loudly and sweating profusely, they both finally laid side by side, holding each other tightly and dozed off as the early morning hours began to heat up and the little house became like a steam bath.

Mia woke up first and said, "Come," and she took Ben, still in the buff, over to the water jar and lovingly washed the sweat off of him. When she finished with Ben, she washed herself off and put on her shorts and told Ben, "You must go. I have to work later and you need to go now, before anyone sees you. Remember what I say, GIs not welcome here. Cholon can be dangerous and we all have been watched by the VC everywhere in my neighborhood. I have seen them."

Ben leaned over and kissed Mia goodbye, little did he know that would be their last encounter, "I'll come to the bar next week and see you again, OK?"

"You my one and only Number One. Yes, you my only one, but you must buy more than one tea or Mama San will fire me."

And with that Ben left, never to see Mia again.

****

Ben rolled over in his bunk, rubbed is eyes, and realized he was wringing wet with sweat. Wes was already sitting on the edge of his bed putting his boots on.

"Are you all right?" he asked Ben, "You were talking in your sleep all night long, moaning and groaning, and carrying on like you were with someone?"

Ben answered, "Yeh, I think I was with someone last night, at least for a little while," he smiled.

"Who's Mia?" Wes responded.

"Jesus, what did I Say?" Ben asked.

"You were carrying on a long running ripe old conversation with someone with that name," he said.

Ben gave him the short, non-sexy part of the story of Mia and said that she was a friend who he helped with her English and she taught him about Vietnamese culture and history---and sex; but he skipped any details of how close they really were.

Wes asked, "So what happened to her anyway? You just finish your tour and leave her there?"

Ben looked at Wes with a little mist in his eyes and told him the rest of the story. Toward the end of his tour the Paris Peace Talks were beginning. He helped with the United Nations damage assessment work from the numerous rocket attacks and other destruction caused by the VC and North Vietnamese. There were rocket and satchel bomb attacks being carried out all over Saigon and surrounding areas.

Once again, Ben learned the rockets were actually being launched from somewhere in the jungle across the Saigon River near their compound. At night, you could hear the rockets going overhead, as they made *whisper* sounds like, *whew, whew, whew,* as they went over Bens barracks and slammed into the city, somewhere.

"So," Ben said to Wes, "one day while I was looking at the latest aerial photography of where the rockets were landing, it became evident to me that most were landing in the Cholon area. The VC and NVA hated the Chinese and targeted that section a lot. I looked at those latest photos. I was totally shocked, as I could make out a familiar part of Cholon. It was the area around the alley that I walked down to get to Mia's place."

He sighed! "And," he continued, "I could see where it ran into the canal. But shit, when I went to look where her house should be, there was nothing left but rubble. Her little house was gone, just large pieces of tin and pieces of wood and rubble, and it stretched along that pathway to a dozen or so other huts, all completely wiped off the face of the earth, there was nothing.

Her whole little neighborhood of tiny little shacks was absolutely wiped out. They must have been hit with more than one rocket. I went back to the restaurant bar where she worked after things calmed down and we were allowed to go back into the city. I was told she just disappeared, end of that story, I am afraid," Ben stated in a very shaky voice.

"Enough of this shit," he said, "I gotta get ready to go to work, and so do you."

CHAPTER 22

Ben and West finished breakfast, and Randy popped in and asked, "No word yet on Rob, shit, I mean Aaron? It's been almost two weeks and not a damn explanation of anything?"

"Nothing," Wes responded. " I just don't get it. How can anyone disappear off the face of the earth like that, especially in this county where everyone knows what everyone else is doing. And shit, Aaron, or whatever his name really is, is such a gawd damn greenhorn, I do not get how he can survive anywhere. He must be holed up in someone's empty house or some abandoned shack; he sure as Hell couldn't survive out in the woods."

Just then, the wall phone clanged out two longs a short and another long, and Randy grabbed the phone. He talked in a quiet voice to whoever was the other end for a good five minutes.

He hung up the phone and then surprised the boys with, "Guess what girls? You know most of the

West has been having large fires, well right now they are running out of crews and equipment. John just told me the Forest is going to send a mop-up crew to a fire in Washington. They want the crews to go up there to free up some of the more experienced crews that have been stuck on mop-up and replace them with project crews like us. We will put a crew together, 15-20 of us from the district and head up there tomorrow."

Ben looked at Wes, "Wow, that is amazing. But Randy, are we qualified to do that?"

"Listen," Randy replied, "we have all been to Guard School. We have put out several lightning fires, and we know how to do mop-up. Every one of you have been on those small fires, so this should be easy. The hard work is done. The fire is essentially contained, so all we will do is just patrol, keep an eye out for fire near the line, and put out all smoke, a chain or two inside the fire line—simple—right?"

Randy continued, "So far the plan is for us to load up all our tools, five or six cases of C-rations, canteens, bedrolls, and then we will drive over to Beeton to the airport and catch a plane to Central Washington. They have some six packs waiting for us to use that are parked at the airstrip."

Any thought of their missing crewmember quickly disappeared, at least for now, as they all went about getting their packs ready for tomorrow's big adventure.

****

The District crew loaded up three six-pack Dodge pickups and were out on the road early, heading to the airport at Beeton. There was Bill, Wes, Ben, Kahuna, and Chris, all excited for a new experience and this time they would be teamed up with engineering crewmembers and other guys on the District making up a 16-person mop-up crew. They also could be called upon to respond to any small new lightning fires if needed.

They arrived at Beeton airport and there on the one long runway was a white DC4 with a black stripe down the middle and *Western Fire* written in bold letters across the upper middle of the fuselage.

"Wow, would you look at that," Kahuna blurted out.

They approached the plane and a loadmaster showed them where to place their tools and gear, and then escorted them around to front of the plane. There were several rows of seats inside, stacks of water and other supplies behind the last row of seats, and, lo and behold, two stewardess-type young ladies.

The plane quickly filled up with another crew that had been at the airport for the last two days. They all loaded in and the two loud engines fired up and they taxied out.

"Shit," the boys heard one of the two attractive young stewardesses, softly exclaim.

"What's the problem?" Kahuna blurted out," thinking he would be real nice and perhaps get her phone number.

"I forgot my darn belt and my jeans are about to fall off."

Kahuna quickly reached into his carry-on pack and pulled out a piece of nylon rope, and said, "Here, take this and tie your pants on, we wouldn't want any embarrassing accidents at 15,000 feet., would we?"

Everyone laughed a little, as she threaded the rope through her belt loops and tied her new belt with a bow. "Thanks, she said, I'll see that you boys are comfortable on this flight.

The plane rumbled slowly down the runway, fully loaded, moving awkwardly like a weirdly gaited camel with wings bouncing, as they rolled down the pitted asphalt runway. The plane seemed to take forever as it slowly started leaving the earth behind, climbing at a snail's pace into the morning sky. The excited firefighters strained to see out the windows as they slowly rose above the fields and forests, finally leaving Beeton behind. They continued the slow ascent, circled around and headed North.

The two nice young ladies brought the boys some water and snacks, to take the edge off of a very bumpy flight. The morning was heating up and thermals were pitching the airplane around quite a bit. But thankfully, it didn't take more than a couple hours for the Captain to come on and announce they were going to land in about 30 minutes.

Ben looked out the window, but all he saw was deep, hilly canyons, no sign of civilization, and definitely no airport. They flew a little while longer and then the plane began a quick descent, bouncing around like on a bucking bronco. It went first sideways and then bounced up and down. Suddenly, they began a quick bank to the right.

Ben looked down, almost straight down the wing as the plane was banking. There below in the bottom of one of the hilly canyons was a single, long, line; the runway. He could see it snake along the canyon bottom and surround by steep sidewalls on both sides. At the upper end of the runway, he could see a bunch of trucks and some people standing around piles of equipment; pumps, hoses, and other supplies.

Ben looked over at Wes and the boys and pondered, "I have no friggin' clue how we are going to land in that canyon."

Just as he spoke, the landing gear and wheels were lowered abruptly with a loud thump. The DC4 quickly descended to a precariously low altitude, dropping down right off the deck a few hundred feet above the canyon walls, along the runway the opposite direction, heading downstream toward an area where the terrain flattens out. Then out of nowhere, the pilot quickly and sharply banked the plane an absolute 180 degrees and dropped the last few hundred feet, swinging around in a tight flightpath. He plopped the DC4 down for a perfect landing on the beginning of the narrow runway and maneuvered the plane in for a safe landing.

Wes looked over at Kahuna and said, "man, I thought I was going to shit my pants!" Everyone laughed out loud in a somewhat muted and fear-dampening response. I cannot believe we just 180'ed that landing the opposite direction and plopped this sucker down inside this steep canyon.

CHAPTER 23

The two crews rolled off the plane, still a little shaken at the roller coaster landing, and went around to the back luggage compartments and started pulling out their gear and stacking it up alongside the pick-ups that were waiting for them. Keys were on the back-rear tire as instructed, and the local District Fire Control Officer was there letting them know where they were going and provided maps for each vehicle with their destination clearly marked. He grabbed Randy who was the "senior" member of the group and briefed him on what fire they would be working on, and the fact that there were three major fires just on this one Forest.

****

Down the runway, away from the off-loaded supplies and nervous crews, Ben noticed cameras and some type of film crew. Ben yelled over to the District

161

Fire guy, "what's with the Hollywood film stuff going on?

"It is a for some new show, I think it is for Disney's Wide world of Color or something like that," he answered. Guys from the fire crews went over and watched as cameras were filming a group of firefighters sharpening their power saws and hand tools. The camera operator was a typical hippie-looking "Hollywood" dude, long hair, colorful shirt, wild looking boots, and some kind of brightly colored tie-dyed style jeans. He was totally engrossed in his filming as he swatted back his hair away from the lens.

****

Someone from one of the crews came over started talking with the camera guy as he was changing film and pretty soon there was a lot of yelling and cussing going on. He was a contract cameraman from New Jersey and not used to being out on location. Next thing you know this guy from one of the crews, a faller, cranks up his chainsaw and starts chasing the cameraman down the runway, revving his saw full throttle the entire time he was chasing him. Ben, Bill, and Wes were right there watching the whole thing in absolute amazement.

"Holy Shit, Wes exclaimed, I wonder what the hell that was that all about?" Just then the District Fire guy came running up toward the two protagonists and stopped them both in their tracks and then proceeded to chew them out, big time, for ten solid minutes.

He was still pissed as he walked back to his pickup and Bill asked him., "what the heck just happened here, do these two know each other?" The District Fire Officer quickly retorted, "Seems like the camera dude said something to the effect the saw guy looked like some kind of Paul Bunyan wannabe with a large dose of hick thrown in. Asked him if he spoke English or just one-syllable logger talk and asked him when the last time was, he took a shower. That was about all he was going to take and told him he better run for his Goddamn life or lose everything below the knees—and off they went, power saw revving all the way. He pretty much scared the wadding out of the guy, but perhaps maybe a little bit of over reaction," as he kind of chuckled a little.

With runway entertainment over, the Blue Mtn Forest crews hopped into their loaded six-packs and headed up the mountain toward their ultimate destination, the Knife Fork Fire. It was named after Knife Fork Creek where the fire originated. It would take them about 45 minutes to an hour to get to where they would hike into the part of the fire line they would mop up, patrol, and generally monitor as their assigned section.

It was about 11:30 when they arrived, and they gathered up their equipment and some C's for a late lunch and started hiking through a large earlier burned area of the forest. They hiked through a thick stand of Lodgepole Pine which was completely blackened. All you could see was burned-out trees void of most of their needles. The whole hillside looked like a bunch of black telephone poles. Any brush or grass that was there originally was now completely wiped out as the fire burned so hot, it burned the litter in many places clear down to bare mineral soil.

It took them about an hour to walk through that part of the fire and you could still see stumps burning and some smoke. It had only burned a couple days earlier. After they arrived near the edge of the fire, they stopped for a quick lunch of C-rations. The day was warming up quickly.

Wes looked around at the terrain where they were sitting and asked Randy, "is this a safe place to be right now?" The reason he asked was they were actually on the edge where the fire stopped, but in this saddle where they were sitting, active fire could be clearly seen some distance downhill from them. It had burned the area they had just walked through behind them, then turned for some unknown reason, perhaps wind shift, and burned up the ridge to their right, leaving a large, unburned island below them. It looked to be around 100 acres of still unburned overstory trees and heavy brush. Further down the mountainside, they could see smoke starting to rise a little higher than when they first arrived. They had one two-channel radio with them and were monitoring what little radio chatter they could hear.

Randy, who was the most experienced and had been in deep thought quickly warned, "look guys, the mop-up work here looks pretty easy, just make sure if you have to move any burning debris, that you flip it back into the black, not downhill. We should be safe especially since we have that large safety area in the black that we just walked through to get here, but just keep a heads up for any wind shifts. That heavy smoke coming from below us could carry some flying embers; so watch for any flare ups or burning embers near the line."

With that the boys went to work; it was a long slow and hot afternoon as they continued putting out all the small flareups and smokes within two chains of the fire line. They widened the fire line in areas where needed and all the time made sure one person was above them at all times acting as a lookout. They stopped about 3:30 and took a break as they had completed quite a bit of the mop up they were assigned to complete during their shift. Wes and Bill returned from patrolling a quarter mile up and down the fire line each way from where the crew was working.

"Nothing out of the ordinary, Bill stated, but we did notice the smoke was quite a bit darker straight down below us. You can't quite see it from here because it's not showing like a huge, tall plume above the trees."

Randy spoke up quickly, "Ok we are now in the part of the day with the most dangerous burning conditions, it's dry, getting hotter by the hour, and I can feel the wind picking up just a little, so let's be damn careful of what we are doing, no dumb moves, keep an eye out for quick changes."

The radio operator, one of the engineering crewmembers yelled over to Randy, "a lot more radio traffic than earlier, Randy, sounds like parts of the fire are getting very active." As they all looked around the fire line and downhill toward the unburned island, they heard a radio report of the possibility of a crew getting cut off or burned over from the now active fire.

Randy looked down hill and his heart took a long pause and with a lump in his throat said, "Shit, I think they are talking about us. Look way down there toward the bottom of that unburned area. Look at the plume of smoke. Just in the last few minutes, it has started rising to where we can now all see the damn thing."

The wind was starting to blow and the boys could see flames in the distance below them and off to their left and right.

"Son of a bitch Randy shouted, Wes, you and Bill go down each section of the line you were on earlier and tell everyone to hightail it back here, NOW!"

Although the crew was spread out, they were not far away and Bill and Wes herded them all back to Randy and Ben's location.

Now they could see trees torching below them and the wind was now hitting around 10-20 mph pushing the fire straight up the hill toward them with fingers continuing to burn off to their left and right, the same area where they had been working.

The noise was getting louder and the fire was crowning out across the entire unburned island below them as Randy shouted, "follow me back the way we came into this area, we should be safe in the black. Call them on the radio to let them know we are all heading into the safety zone in the black and we will hike back to our rigs." Soon, all the crew was inside the safety of the previously burned out and blackened safe area and they began hiking back. By now, the entire 100 plus acre area was totally engulfed in flames reaching as high as a hundred feet above the treetops and sounding like a half dozen freight trains screaming out of control. They quickly picked up the pace as they hiked several hundred feet inside the burned-out forest, but now they had a new problem. As quickly as that fire spread, the wind had picked up just as fast, and it was now blowing a steady 25-35 miles per hour and felt like it was gusting as high as 50 for brief moments.

"Shit, Wes yelled over the sound of the increasing winds, this is not a very good place to be right now. The fire area might have been safer."

"Why is that?" Ben asked. Before Wes could answer the question, they all heard a loud **whoosh**, **crash**, and one of the burnt-out snags nearby came crashing to the ground.

Randy gathered the entire crew around him and cautioned, "Look, I'm not going to gloss this over, this could be the most dangerous one-mile hike we ever have to do. There is little if any soil anchoring these burned-out trees to the ground, and to top it off the wind is getting worse so just about any of these trees could blow down at anytime, anywhere, watch your stop and watch your heads. We'll take that same deer trail back to the rigs, it's only about a mile or aa little less."

Off they went winding back toward the rigs along that deer trail they entered on. The trail was rocky in places at times full of tree roots. There were several places where the trail became very narrow as it wound through the blackened skeleton of a forest. Up front the radio operator stopped for a second to answer a call and as he turned around and started walking **whoosh. Crash...,** and everyone heard the sound as a 50-foot tall lodgepole blew over and struck him squarely on the right shoulder knocking the radio 10 feet away. Randy, Wes, and Ben were right behind him and quickly started looking under the tree to see if he was alive. "Jesus Christ, Wes cried out, he's bleeding real bad. There's a big gash on the right side of his head."

Randy yelled, "go grab that faller, his crew was right behind us, get him up here quick, we have got to get this weight off of him, but be careful."

With the saw kicking out sawdust as the second cut was completed, the crew quickly picked up a short log off the fallen body as Randy checked for a pulse. "Bring that first aid kit over here, pull out the large compresses and tape and we'll dress the wound as best we can. I think I do feel a pulse. Bill, you head back to where we parked," Randy shouted above the wind. The District has a first tent set up down there, see if they can radio for an ambulance or helicopter for evac. We need to get this guy to a hospital now, he is lost an awful lot of blood in a very short time. We better not move him unless this wind gets even more dangerous and we have to move or get hit by another tree."

Suddenly, the wind subsided just as quickly as it came up an hour earlier and everyone huddled around their fallen crewmember just as Bill arrived with two guys from the First Aid tent. They had a stretcher and another radio. Bill looked at Randy, "how is he? Is he going to be OK?"

Randy quickly replied with an uncharacteristically shaky voice, "Not sure, he's lost a lot of blood. Let's get him out of here. He has a very faint pulse." Bill glanced at the medic guys, "OK to go?"

The lead first aide responder answered, "We have ordered a helicopter and it should land at the parking area in about 15-20 minutes, that should be good timing with four of us each grabbing a corner of the litter and getting the hell out of here before the wind picks up again; let's get going."

As the four litter bearers carefully but swiftly wound their way through the blackened forest, they could hear the helicopter land just as they reached the opening at the parking area. He was quickly loaded onto the attached stretcher and the Ex-Vietnam helicopter pilot wasted no time climbing, banking, and heading toward the nearest hospital, some 25 minutes flight time away. By now it was almost six in evening and everyone looked at each other, the blood from the radio operator was on their pants and shirts, and most of the crew slumped to the ground, all fighting back tears. It was a day they would wish they could forget, but everyone knew they never would.

The local District Fire Officer drove up quickly and approached the crew. "You guys did a helluva job out there under one of the most dangerous circumstances most of us will never see in our careers. Right now, he appears somewhat stable and I just heard they are about ten minutes out from the hospital. The emergency room is standing by with a trauma team including an ER surgeon and anyone else they need. I won't lie, his chances are not all that good, but without your quick attention, he would be dead now. You guys really did do a great job out there today, even if the fire did wipe out some of your work. Although you guys are still needed here, I am cutting orders for you and the other crew to go home late tomorrow morning. Going through this kind of trauma is not easy and the fire line is not the place for you guys right now. I have rooms reserved in town for you tonight. In situations like this, you need to decompress and just get home to your friends, family, and crewmembers, OK?"

Everyone kind of nodded as the immensity of what just happened suddenly sunk in and the fact his chances were not that good made the mood even more dark.

****

Early the next morning, some of the crew were up early, out for a run; some were out just walking around. For breakfast, the two crews were fed in two different restaurants, but the mood was still overshadowed by the events of yesterday. Breakfast was not on their minds as they picked and poked at their food. "Look," Randy stated to the crew, "what we did yesterday was pretty damned amazing when you think about it. I didn't know the guy very well, actually not at all. His name is Jim and we never see him much because he lives on a ranch a couple miles from the work center and his engineering guys pick him up every morning on the way out. Since he's local, and from a well-known family, we may be getting a lot of questions. I suggest everyone just refer any questions about his condition to the family and any questions about what happened to me unless you are OK answering."

"Any word on his condition?" one of the guys asked.

Randy started to smile just a little and answered, "Glad you asked because I was told earlier this morning Jim is alert, awake, and can actually sit up on the edge of his bed. He had over a dozen stitches to his scalp and a couple broken ribs when he fell on the root wad. But, that radio that was slung over his shoulder, took most of the impact of the tree. The radio caused that tree to slightly glance away just enough to avoid what surely could have been critical head injuries. It sounds like he will be able to go home in 3-5 days. If asked, like I said earlier, refer his condition to the family or here to the hospital."

CHAPTER 24

Later that morning the DC 4 brought the two crews back to Beeton and they immediately loaded up their parked rigs with their gear and headed back home, home to Mineral Creek, their home away from yesterday. "You know what," Ben offered, it's been over a month and we haven't even hardly talked about what happened to Rob, I mean Aaron. Not a word from his father, not a word from Sgt. Dusty, what do you suppose is going on?" I wonder if they still think I might have shoved him off that log?" he asked. Damnit, I didn't, and you guys know that, right-RIGHT?"

Randy looked over and replied, "if they thought there was any funny business or a crime, trust me, you guys would have been quickly brought back to the station answering questions from one side of the bars or the other."

As Ben started to relax a little in the back seat, he watched the country roll by. He noticed all the tin hay barns and other tin shacks and his mind wandered once again back to Vietnam. He remembered why he had extended his tour an extra two months. If he had less than 90 days of military service after his tour ended, he could, he could get an early out, get discharged, and go home. Besides the big Tet offensive that made international news, he started to remember that one day of his tour of duty in particular, a day of another VC offensive, a day that brought the war even closer to him.

****

Ben remembered that day clearly as he was leaving the Intelligence Center to catch their usual bus, the "green monster" as they nicknamed it, back to the barracks. Ben's new bunkmate Phil rushed up slightly out of breath and said, "something has gone wrong, there are no busses coming, just deuce and halves. I didn't hear why, but it sounds like there could be another big trouble once again all around Saigon and the surrounding countryside."

Just then, the trucks rolled into the area parking area at the front entrance to the center. They were the typical version of a deuce and a half, except these had the wooden seats removed that used to go along both sides of the bed. The driver was armed to the teeth, and his shotgun had an automatic weapon of some type and enough ammo for half a war.

"Everyone count off as you get in, I want only 14 people in each deuce and a half. I want seven of you to get up close to each of the metal side walls as you can on both sides and keep your Goddamn heads down until I tell you it's ok."

"Jesus, Phil clamored, what the Hell is happening?"

They would find out soon enough. As they left the driveway onto the traffic circle to Highway 1, it was soon evident that all hell was about to or had already broken loose. The streets were absolutely empty. There were no mama sans carrying baskets, no cycles, pedicabs, motorbikes, or bicycles. There wasn't but one or two locals out on the street. Quiet streets like this happened several times this past year Ben thought and always when the VC were in the area. They turned off the highway onto the back road toward their compound as the driver yelled, "OK, reminder time, keep your damn heads all the way down and don't try to get up or look around!" He put the deuce and a half in high gear and hauled ass as fast the engine's governor would allow, bouncing all over the narrow road.

Ben could see what used to be the tin buildings, storefronts, homes, and then some of the nicer two-story homes made out of stucco and block and then more tin-roofed stores. Then suddenly, Ben could see huge chunks of tin that was blown all over the area and all those shacks were now completely leveled. The two-story stucco homes they were passing all had smoke in the upper windows pouring out and there were bullet holes and RPG damage all over them.

They approached their compound and Ben looked over at Phil and stammered, "Shit, did you see that- "two story" is gone and so is the sawmill across the street." The four trucks rolled into the quickly opened front gates and Ben looked back across the country road at the completely leveled sawmill and "two-story." Two-story was the nickname for the infamous bar and whorehouse where you could go right out the front gate and have a beer and spend some time with the ladies, usually a visit which resulted in the need for lots of penicillin. It was totally flattened and unrecognizable.

Inside the compound back by their barracks was a rather large tank from the Big Red 1. It was parked just a few feet from the Saigon River, in between the two barracks with its main gun pointed toward at the area across the river toward the jungle area surrounding the island. You could hear sporadic gunfire not too far away and as Ben started to say something to Phil, a Cobra gunship arrived on the scene and was immediately overhead firing off several short bursts with casings flying everywhere. No one saw what the ship was firing at, but as Ben thought to himself later, *I am sure glad they were there.*

Now that they were safely inside the perimeter of their compound, they looked across toward the large sawmill that had been completely destroyed and they could see and hear what looked like a distant firefight. Small arms fire and an occasional burst from an M-16 continued from time to time. A couple A1 Skyraiders appeared overhead, approaching the area behind the sawmill. These old training planes were still in use by the South Vietnamese Air Force and they could hold a single thousand-pound bomb or two five hundred bombs, and they were amazingly accurate. The first Skyraider flew around the back of the compound at around 3,000 feet in elevation, circled over the old sawmill, and then suddenly dove straight down and at about a 1,000 feet or so off the deck, he released his two 500 hundred-pound bombs just before he took a hard-right bank. The concussion was so close, Ben could feel it hit the pit of his stomach and the explosions and noise that followed rattled his head. The second plane repeated the same drop with explosions occurring followed by flying debris in an area behind the mill site, and then silence. No gun fire, no more explosions, nothing. A couple hours later, the tank rumbled out the front gate and inside the compound things returned to "normal."

Normal was never going to be the same as for the next two months or more, the bus trips had an armed escort, front and rear. But gradually, things did normalize as the NCO club at the back of the compound re-opened, and the 15 cent beer once again flowed like the river next door.

Ben's ever-occurring daydreams were interrupted when Randy gruffly asked, "Ben are you with us or are you somewhere else, what the Hell are you daydreaming about now?"

Ben sheepishly replied, "just thinking about things I don't like thinking about. Why don't you turn on the radio since we have one in this rig and we are only 30 minutes out we should pick up our local station?" Randy turned on the radio and the boys settled in for some music when all of a sudden the local announcer came on and started reading a news bulletin live on the air. Live news was very rare and only happed during an emergency or when the usual taped stuff did cut it. It was pretty obvious this guy was not what you would call a pro on the air.

But when the news switched quickly from country music a rather non-professional announcer broke in, *"And now an up to the minute news bulletin from here in Riverton. The Sheriff's office has just announced that a body has been discovered in the millpond West of town."*

"Turn that up, Ben yelled. What did he say about a body?"

All of a sudden everyone got quiet and then Bill asked the obvious, "Do you think they found Rob, er, I mean Aaron, shit, I wonder what the hell happened?"

They all stopped talking and listened intently to see if any other information about the discovery was in the newscast.

The announcer paused a little and then continued, *"according to still yet unconfirmed reports, it looks like this could be the body of the missing Forest Service greenhorn that local law enforcement officers have been investigating for the last month or so. We have no further information at this time as everyone is on-scene right now. We will try and get an interview over there at the mill site as soon as we can get someone out there. We will go back to our regular programming, but we'll break in if any new updates are available."*

"I can't believe we were just talking about this a few minutes ago and now this news report, wonder what the story is," Wes thought out load.

Ben responded, "not sure but we are going to find out whether we want to or not. I can't believe after what we went through these past several days, our return back home ends like this. But I am glad we might finally have some answers if that is in fact Aaron they found."

"Who the Hell else would it be, West blurted out. There's only been one person gone missing in this little burg in the last hundred years. Shit who else would it be, that old geezer in the guard shack."

As they continued into town, Randy offered, " hey look since we are here by the District Office, let's all go and turn our timeslips in, especially since we had a few extra hours on the fire, well more like a couple extra hours?"

The boys were more than a little tired and still a little shaky from their fire experience and then that radio news bulletin really go to them. As they walked into the District Office, Helen, the District Clerk, asked, "You boys OK, what brings you in to the Office?"

Randy answered, "Since we are on our way through town, we thought we would go ahead and drop off our time slips and make it a little easier on you to have them early."

179

Before Helen could reply, Ranger Bash rushed into the reception area and stated emphatically, "Ben, you and Wes and Bill are wanted over in Sgt Dusty's office. He and the Sheriff would like a few words with you. They finished at the mill site about an hour ago. Randy, you can go along with them if you want."

"Shit," Wes said, "what the hell now, we have been through enough the last couple days and now this crap, we need to just get back to the work center and get some damn sleep."

The boys loaded up and headed over to the police station without a word between them. When they arrived Randy asked, "Do you want me to stay here or come in with you guys?"

"Hell," Wes blurted out, "who cares who's in there come on in, you might as well hear first-hand what he wants before the radio blabs it all over the damn place."

Sgt. Dusty was near the front door with the Sheriff and politely stated, "come on in and I'll let you know what we found out about your friend Aaron.

"Here's the deal, when the mill workers were lifting up a large pine log, they could see something under it as it started coming out of the water."

They immediately shut down the conveyor and went around to see what it was. Underneath the partially submerged log, was Aaron's body. The cold water left him in good condition and enabled the coroner to make a quick preliminary determination of cause of death.

"What happened," Ben asked. How could he possibly end up underneath a log in the pond and no one saw him, not the divers, not even the watchman or workers?"

"No sure about that," the Sgt. replied. "Here's what we do know. This particular log had some barbed wire from what we think might have been someone's range allotment fence. Some of the wire was still attached to the log underneath. The faller probably missed it when he bucked up the tree. That along with a couple small branch knots somehow seems to have ended up entangled with Aaron's clothing. What it looks like is he somehow slide off the log and tried to come back up but got snagged by the wire and short pieces of a couple branches that weren't cut flush. It is highly doubtful you guys would have heard or seen anything with all the thunder and lightning that night and then the lights going off and on."

"But what about the hounds tracking a scent on the other side; they tracked him away from and then back to the edge of the pond,' Bill Asked?

Sgt Dusty responded, "You guys were looking for him for a good half hour before you ended up at the pond. We think that during that time he probably just wandered around back and forth and then climbed on a log over on the other side and somehow drifted or paddled over toward the guard shack. It was a little windy that night and that might have helped his movement. It wasn't that far, even on the water."

"Look boys, the coroner his ruled his death as an accidental drowning, probably as a result of prescription drugs mixed with alcohol. His father pretty much agreed with that when we talked with him a few minutes ago. He was pretty shook up, but I somehow got the feeling that he was not surprised. Aaron's father stated emphatically that his son was told to never drink while taking his prescription medicines. The body was in good shape and the coroner could see nothing physical to indicate his finding of accidental drowning was any different. The only thing he noticed on the body was some trauma on the right side of his head, but he thinks that was from bumping into the log as he tried to free himself. Odd shape though, almost round. All right boys, unless you have any questions, you are all free to go back to Mineral Creek, I doubt if I need anything else from any of you."

They headed back up the mountain, mostly in silence. Wes in an unusually quiet voice asked, "Do you guys really think it's over? It just seems the coroner was damn quick with his findings."

"Yeh," Randy responded, "but remember, the coroner here is not a medical examiner, and he can decide enough is enough and just go with his gut feeling. There's only one doctor in town now and I doubt he has time to disagree. I think he probably already signed the off on the cause of death. But I gotta tell you, I am really wondering about them finding that something caused "head trauma" as he called it. Especially the fact that it was somewhat round-shaped.

"Shit!" And then Bill choked out the question on everyone's mind; damn, "Ben did you hit---did you cold-cock Aaron with the end of that pike pole. I remember you shoved the damn thing out there pretty dog gone hard?"

Ben looked over at Bill with a slightly evil-looking half smile, and said, "You know what, I…"

The End

NOTE FROM THE AUTHOR KEN PALMROSE

This book took five years to write. For decades, I rarely admitted to anyone that I was a Vietnam Vet or what I did during my tour of duty. As a non-combatant, it was hard, if not downright embarrassing for me to talk about the easy times I enjoyed the first seven months of my tour. This was especially true considering my friends, colleagues, and classmates that experienced the horrors of combat, several of which were wounded not only physically, but mentally as well. and of course, those who never came home. But for me, the war itself finally did become a stark reality as the attacks of the 1968 Tet and May offensives hit close to home.

There were many people I worked with during my 36-year with the USDA-Forest Service career that knew me, some for 25 years, and didn't realize I was a Vietnam Vet. I chose to ignore, maybe even forget my service, and never admit it. Now, after much discussion with many whom I consider real heroes and thanks to their heartfelt expressions of appreciation for my service, I am actually proud of being a Vietnam Vet and what I accomplished.

This book is a fiction piece but at times is loosely based on actual events and incidents. It is a reminder that no matter what happens in a war zone, the memories do not fade away---- ever.